Praise for *Childre*

Five Stars. *Children of Tomorrow* is an essential read. An emotionally heavy one, but with plenty of pay-off. Both along the way—the beautiful prose, the projected new technologies and creativity of human beings when facing the worst—and in the end, with the offer and acknowledgement that, in some form at least, things will continue.—MEGAN PAYNE, ARTS HUB (AUSTRALIA)

Intimate and profound, *Children of Tomorrow* is a love song for a burning planet.—JAMES BRADLEY, AUTHOR OF *CLADE*

With echoes of Kim Stanley Robinson, James Bradley and Richard Powers, JR Burgmann provides a lyrical catalogue of the terrifying crises to come. If you're waiting for a hero to save us, *Children of Tomorrow* is a timely reminder that climate change is caused by a complex network of people, and that collective action and diverse approaches are our only way out of this.—JANE RAWSON, AUTHOR OF *A WRONG TURN AT THE OFFICE OF UNMADE LISTS*

In *Children of Tomorrow*, JR Burgmann delivers a pre-emptive elegy to our world as it spins through the 21st century into what could conceivably be the human race's endgame. The tension increases chapter by chapter much like the carbon dioxide in the air, preventing characters, and us, from breathing easily. And yet, as resources dwindle, stability vanishes and long-held values and viewpoints fall by the wayside, the relationships and networks that bind us to each other in our inevitably shared destiny hold, just about, though not without cost, and certainly not without grief. This novel doesn't pull its punches but does, ultimately, nail its colours to the mast of that most persistent and valuable of all human commodities: hope.—PAUL DALGARNO, AUTHOR OF *A COUNTRY OF ETERNAL LIGHT*

Children of Tomorrow is a vivid and disturbing vision of what could happen in this coming century if we don't respond well to the current polycrisis. It's not a matter of end-of-everything apocalypse, but rather a continuous epic struggle to cope with wild change. Burgmann shows how the novel can be put back to its proper use describing history itself, by way of braided swift stories of people doing the epic work of survival. A novel to remember!—KIM STANLEY ROBINSON, AUTHOR OF *THE MINISTRY FOR THE FUTURE*

Children of Tomorrow

CHILDREN

of

TOMORROW

J. R. BURGMANN

ENFIELD
&WIZENTY

Enfield & Wizenty (an imprint of Great Plains Press)
320 Rosedale Ave
Winnipeg, MB R3L 1L8
www.greatplainspress.ca
Originally published by Upswell Publishing, Perth, Australia

Great Plains Publications gratefully acknowledges the financial support provided for
its publishing program by the Government of Canada through the Canada Book
Fund; the Canada Council for the Arts; the Province of Manitoba through the
Book Publishing Tax Credit and the Book Publisher Marketing Assistance Program;
and the Manitoba Arts Council.

First Canadian edition
Design & Typography by Relish New Brand Experience
Printed in Canada by Friesens

Library and Archives Canada Cataloguing in Publication

Text on page 112 is excerpted from Greta Thunberg's "Our House is on Fire" speech
at the 2019 World Economic Forum

Title: Children of tomorrow / J.R. Burgmann.
Names: Burgmann, J. R., author.
Description: Previously published: Perth, Western Australia: Upswell Publishing, 2023.
Identifiers: Canadiana 20230472893 | ISBN 9781773371092 (softcover)
Subjects: LCGFT: Novels.
Classification: LCC PR9619.4.B87 C55 2023 | DDC 823/.92—dc23

ENVIRONMENTAL BENEFITS STATEMENT

Great Plains Press saved the following resources by
printing the pages of this book on chlorine free paper
made with 100% post-consumer waste.

TREES	WATER	ENERGY	SOLID WASTE	GREENHOUSE GASES
12	930	5	39	5,040
FULLY GROWN	GALLONS	MILLION BTUs	POUNDS	POUNDS

Environmental impact estimates were made using the Environmental Paper Network
Paper Calculator 4.0. For more information visit www.papercalculator.org

Canada

FSC
www.fsc.org
MIX
Paper from
responsible sources
FSC® C016245

For Norah and Hadley
May this world not be your own

*To be human is to confuse a satisfying story with
a meaningful one, and to mistake life for something huge
with two legs. No: life is mobilized on a vastly larger scale,
and the world is failing precisely because no novel
can make the contest for the world seem as compelling
as the struggles between a few lost people.*
—Richard Powers, *The Overstory*

Contents

There used to be so much colour in the world.

It burst from beneath your feet and filled the Earth and its oceans and its skies. It was everywhere, but we did not see the miracle. You could hold infinite marvels in your hand—the way Arne does a fading gumleaf now—and peer into their nature.

Sitting on his haunches, spinning the leaf by its frail stem, he considers the empty shoreline. He rises to his feet and hobbles down to the water, wading in up to his knees, which click and creak with every movement. He scans the quiet cove, and beyond—the empty, darkening horizon.

He moves further out, deeper.

He places the gumleaf on the water and, after a time, lets it go. It floats like a magic carpet, rising and falling on the sea, drifting away.

He waits.

Time flickers, and at some darker hour he gives up, hauling his failing body back to the land, heaving painfully as he climbs the crumbling beach and reaches the gumrest, a place where he ought to sit and rest and forget all the years. But instead, as he waits for his dearest, his chronicling mind winds back through the past, remembering the century.

CENTURY'S
BEGINNING

1

EXTINCTION

Carbon dioxide parts per million: 402.5

Sunset on the mountaintop and the lake goldens, shimmering purple out to its bank.

'To be more precise,' Thomas begins to his student, 'it's a *tarn*. The formation here is glacial.'

Arne Bakke knows the sound of this word, but not, until now, its meaning. He nods, listening—or, at the very least, appearing to listen. That is very important: appearing to listen to your supervisor. 'Academics love it,' Wally, his closest friend, had quipped over drinks one night, back when Arne was first weighing up whether or not to accept the doctoral scholarship—a meagre sum—he'd been offered. 'They are lonely, increasingly irrelevant creatures. On the verge of extinction. No one gives a fuck about research,' Wally had continued, before emphatically gulping his beer, sacrificing his Quebecois beard to a snowy cloud of foam. 'Just remember that, Arnie. The world will not care about what you do. It won't even pretend to listen. At the very least pretend to listen to your supervisor.' But now, as they amble along the boardwalk that encloses the tarn, Arne finds that he is in fact listening to the professor, and the professor to him.

Around them, the world is afire with life. Dusky robins arc like darts through the air and alight on the posts of the boardwalk, chirruping to each other. Yellow wattlebirds—the largest of the honeyeaters—venture out from their banksia havens and rattle off bronchial songs. From on high, a cacophony of black currawongs undulates across the fading mauve sky, laughing wildly. A wombat mother with her gambolling joey scutter behind a mound to wait for these two humans, who have interrupted their snuffling about the peatland, to piss off.

The weeks here have awakened something in him. Something dangerous: a desire, green and budding, to know a wordless world. Out here among the alpine eucalypts, he has been tuning himself down to the lowest frequency he can muster, going slow, unknotting ancient burls of meaning. He hardly makes a dent when drilling an increment borer apologetically into the core of a great swamp gum, those impossibly large and flowering miracles that touch the sky and deliver down expansive understories. Each time Arne extracts those neat cylinders of tissue, there is no telling what his auger has done to the tree: what he has taken.

Arne has begun to learn how to read trees, those great columns of planetary history, locking climate's rising tale in latewood. The rings there tell stories—longstanding sagas, dispensed in annual episodes of varying length and quality. They are intricate productions, staged for no one in particular but telling all.

The immense beings with which Arne and Professor Thomas Hadley—along with two other research assistants—have spent the past few weeks are, at one hundred to one hundred and fifty years old, mere tender sprouts. Although nothing in the vast calendar of geology, they outstrip the fleshy lives of these prodding people many times over. They have coiled cousins, angled aunts and troublesome grandfather trees elsewhere across Tasmania with even deeper roots, older stories—far beyond the roots of words—engrained deep into their heartwoods. Grand encyclicals within their trunks, dividing the good years from the bad, divining seasons cruel and kind, each change of climate accounted for and augured in wood's delicate script.

It occurs to Arne, ambling along the boardwalk by the tarn, that the old man beside him—who, rather fittingly, will live to one

hundred and three and die saving a tree—has more in common
with trees than with men. Maybe he's going mad, but the professor
always seems to travel great distances without moving his branchy
body much at all. His stillness is swaying, unwavering yet willowy.
He can get birds to land on his shoulder. He knows exactly where
a tree's shadow will rise and fall across the day, the month, the
year. When he talks, low woodwind semibreves, muffled beneath
a greying canopy of moustache, rise mysteriously into the air. And
where others hear a broad Yorkshire accent, Arne is certain he is
hearing words spoken by the most treely of men.

'How are you, lad?' Thomas asks.

Arne pauses to look out across the gleaming water, the light
playing scarily religious tricks. 'Fine,' he lies.

'That all? Just fine.'

'Yep.'

Thomas nods, exhaling slowly, deeply. 'I think, after a year of
knowing you, I can tell when things are…askew.'

'Okay…'

'It's your family, isn't it?'

'What?' Arne says, alarmed.

'Your family. Home. Being back in Tassie again after…what?'

'Four years.'

'That's quite some time. Particularly when you've only been
on the mainland. It's not like Melbourne's the other side of the
world.' For Arne, it might as well have been. 'Do you ever talk
to him—your dad?'

'Not much.'

'What about your brother, the activist—what's his name?'

'Freddie.'

'Right, Freddie. I remember. Does he talk to him at all?'

Arne shakes his head.

The professor pauses, lost in thought, his brow furrowing to
reveal deep grooves, bark skin. A creaking limb extends slowly
around the sapling Arne. 'If you're struggling being back here,

just let me know. I might be better with trees, but I'm not so bad with humans, strange as they are. Well, at least, I'd like to think so. You should try talking to John and Kim. No need to be so guarded, trust me.'

They continue their circuit back towards the campsite. Eager to impress, Arne tries to weave observations of a scientific nature into their evening amble. The limitations of dendrochronology. The horizons of dendroclimatology. The places carbon might best go. Drawdowns, sinks, the future. How things can be used and what can be put where.

Thomas recognises something of himself in Arne. He too was once a sapling. Not wanting to uproot Arne's spirit by telling him that *these beings will all be massacred—deracinated—before then*, Thomas shows Arne something infinitely more valuable: how to see a tree true, and how to best remember them—'Seed storage,' he jokes—when they are gone.

'We don't really know much about the green world,' Thomas begins, digging the heel of his boot into the wooden planking, then he begins to speak of all the curious ways in which trees overhang the lives of lower beings. His knowledge is wide-ranging. His anecdotes branch magnificently, but always stay connected to the trunk of things. Of redwoods who fight fire. Of spikey kapoks who buoyantly shake down large, white-yellow fuzzball seeds that, brought together, can float just about anything. Of a bristlecone pine, Methuselah—older than gods and unimaginatively named, the tree itself being hermaphroditic and bearing a different, truer name among its own kind—which came into being during an age of rising oceans, splendid warmth, and a new fad called agriculture.

Thomas could go on like this forever—and will, in fact, as he, after years of being broken down by fungi and worms and time, will be wholly reabsorbed from the Earth by the same far-off kapok he will save deeper into this century. There is no such thing as a final resting place. But for now, Thomas offers Arne the kindest thing he can to someone who will live through great change: ways to hold still and consider the world as it really is.

Secrets, plainspoken. Of flesh, wood, rock, and fire. *Green goes longer than flesh, rocks longer than trees, stars longer than rocks—all within the cradle of the universe. In reverse, now, from the banging beginning: physics, chemistry, biology.*

'It's not only about science. Science matters, sure. But not to *them.*' Thomas gestures behind Arne, in the direction of the forest. 'We live among *them.* This is their world, and we are visitors stepping briefly out of our own illusion. They already know things we never will. They have lived them. And they will continue to live them when we are gone. It's important not just to take data here, but also meaning. Tell a story, something that matters. *Tree* and *Truth* share the same root.'

Thomas invokes some dead poet Arne does not know: a tree contains multitudes, concealing stories, trading them underground from member to member along mycelial networks, fungal canals pliable for signification—the greatest runners in planetary history— and endless recirculation. As an order, they are the great witnesses of the Earth, telling of something unbearably vast, stretching out backwards and forwards across the great spatial plains of time.

Arne nods, somewhere between listening and pretending to listen, trying to comprehend his supervisor's wood-words. 'These things'—Thomas gestures vaguely in the air—'they are all far greater than each of us alone.' What Arne is taking in—capturing and storing—he isn't sure, but he does catch a leafy calm from the permanence of treekind which Thomas invokes. It's solid as hell. Arne is starting to see how that world is more detailed, more varied, more complex and interconnected, than anything—anyone—with which he has ever shared air.

Maybe he has a people problem. Unlike Freddie, he has never quite been able to figure out the pulse of his own species—cunning, calculating humanity. Their little motives and dreams, such a rapid and unsure thing, ever ticking, ever worrying. But a tree: it will sustain him, hold him by the feet as it would the petiole of a leaf. And he, in turn, feels the crowning sense that he must commit his short life to a slow and wondrous enduring empire—a penance for all the trees he stood by and watched fall, growing up.

LATER THAT NIGHT, around the ochre glow of campfire, Arne begins to mumble and puff oxygen into those strange internal sensations. The fire purges him. The other researchers—John, a Noongar man, thousands of miles from home, and Kim, a Seoul-born woman whose family moved to Melbourne at an inconvenient time in her school years—collapse into laughter, seesawing on their woodlog stumps, teasing Arne the newbie. John ribs him for being so basic: just another white man, unable to deal with common feeling. Kim expresses her agreement in knee slaps and whisky swigs. In the near darkness, beyond the fire's reach, Arne can make out Thomas, silhouetted and swaying in a trunk-strung hammock.

Way up, dull clouds of the night slip away, unveiling the starry sky and casting the old man in brilliant moonglow. The full array of night-time whites and blues, illuminating the gumforest kingdom, encircling the crackling yellow blaze at its centre. Amused by their banter, Thomas rises from his hammock to join them.

It has been a dry summer of bushfires, so, even at this altitude, they manage the fire with great care. Another incendiary season of socially alienated arsonists, natural ignitions and infernal sacrifices. People and gumgods must be sated. And eucalypts, in their own special way, renewed. Ending and beginning in rapturous fire. Rebirth. The invaders of this continent have never really got their heads around this cycle, being bound to colder places, where trees are not primed to explode. See how they ogle as fires rage across the land each and every fire season.

It shouldn't surprise them; it always does. The end of things is always beyond imagination.

Thomas pours everyone a drink, topping up Kim's tin cup—the tinkle of which makes Arne want to go and pee behind a tree four times over—and, testing the greenest of his protégés, divulges to John and Kim how the skinny lad Arne comes from a long line of Tasmanian loggers, burly men who send living, breathing colossi crashing to the ground, stripping and preparing them for all manner of strange modern addictions, afterlives as beautifully inanimate objects. Arne's father and uncle, his grandfather before them. His great-grandfather, and his great-great-grandfather, a Norwegian whaler, who, having arrived one southern autumn on the east coast of Australia in search of humpback, southern right and orca blubber, eventually turned south in search of gold. After failing terribly at that, he carved out a final, desperate lust for lumber on this island.

'That's so badass,' Kim blurts out.

'Huh?' Arne responds.

'That's wild. Colonial as fuck. You couldn't make that shit up.' She's moved on to beer now, indifferent to the codes by which to sequence alcohol.

Arne has gathered that, for a bioengineer and avid coder, Kim is wildly unpredictable. At first her chaos made him anxious. She would pin him down with her laser eyes—often against the trunk of a tree he was assessing—and ask all kinds of dangerous, direct questions. She would crack electrically lewd jokes, as though there were no greater pleasure in the universe than tormenting the simple and sincere. Other times she could be incredibly kind and introspective—or just outright bizarre, as when designating eccentric sobriquets to the gums above them: Lando Bloom, Staunch, Albatross, Skywalker, Treebeard. Eventually, with help from John—who observed all the while that this was a clear instance of settler linguistic violence—and Thomas, they recalled and assigned instead the names of Ents: Finglas, Fladrif, Beechbone, Bregalad, Fimbrethil. Arne didn't know what an Ent was but wanted to find out. John told him not to bother: 'There are better books. Watch the movies if you have to.'

John is a gentle, self-assured enigma. He rarely talks about himself, instead focusing outwards, in search of some perfect phenomenon. He is concise but generous, to the point but thorough. Part philosophy, part botany, John's research is groundbreaking, according to Thomas. Something to do with the destruction of the global climate being the final frontier of colonial expansion. When John reluctantly expanded on this, Arne felt out of his depth, inadequate in the presence of this man's fierce, probing intelligence.

Here, around the campfire, John asks Arne a terrifyingly real question. 'So. How do you feel about it?'

'About what?'

'That history. All that…taking. That extraction.'

Arne knows how he should feel. He drills into himself, boring through the twenty-six rings of his life in search of true growth lines—healthy deposits of shame and self-loathing, guilt and disappointment, developed steadily throughout the years—but finds nothing. Nothing but confusion. Perhaps he is better at reading trees than himself. Or maybe that lineage, so proudly boasted about and chest-beaten around the house by the men of his family, is too difficult to reckon with. Or maybe he is deficient, broken.

He's embarrassed, and the absurd irony of that feeling is not lost on him. 'I feel awful,' Arne tries. It's not an outright lie.

John does not hesitate. 'Bullshit.' He tucks stray locks of dark hair behind his ears. 'Unless you mean you feel awful about not feeling awful.'

Arne turns to Thomas, who looks back at him now, eyebrows raised, clearly enjoying himself. He has the look of a man who has seen this picture umpteen times and knows how it will pan out. He motions, encouraging Arne to go on.

'You're right,' Arne admits.

'Listen,' John says, sighing. 'You can't ever feel awful enough. There's a limit. Lots of vaguely intelligent settler people—invaders —say, "I just feel so awful, so guilty, there must be something I can do." They're looking to make themselves feel better. To absolve their guilt. But they still go home at night, eat dinners cooked and delivered by strangers, watch some shitty American TV, take a shit, have a wank, go to bed, and all while not even knowing the names and meanings of the places they live.'

Thomas cackles. Kim is loving this.

John continues. He starts drawing diagrams through the air only of his knowing. 'The way things are—the way things are set up. There's limited potential and use for such individual feeling.'

Kim leans across John tipsily, pretending to make sense of his tracing hand movements; he repositions himself to hold her up a little, take some of her weight.

'Systems inoculate against it, shut down and detain all kinds of realities. It would take unprecedented social and political transformation—an evolution, a quantum leap—to reckon with the recent history of not only this land, but the planet. And'—he pauses and stares distantly into the fire, two miniature flames now flickering in his eyes—'to face the fuckpile of coming catastrophes.'

Arne tries to take this all in.

John rasps a palm across the stubble of his chin, which, deep in thought, he juts out pensively. 'Just read my thesis,' he says, wry and certain of the world's demise. 'Nobody else will.'

'Oh, I wouldn't be so sure about that,' Thomas offers. 'The world might surprise you.'

'Whatever you say, prof.'

They fall silent for a time. The forest cracks and groans, sends out a susurrus to sound out the four of them. The stars twinkle out here like they never do in cities, lighting up the green world as if daylight were no big deal. Each facet, each spur, each fallen leaf and bed of duff, each rise and fall along the floor of the underwood, each cube of wombat turd, each hustling marsupial, viewable here beneath that primordial light, projected from infinite star clusters, beaming from systems of unknown worlds, long ago, when time was not time.

Kim quite suddenly asks Arne, 'So, what happened?'

'What happened with what?'

'With your family?'

'Well…We sort of ran away. Me and my brother Freddie.'

'No, like, what are they doing now?'

'Logging their way into the Tarkine. Opening it up for mining. We grew up close to there.'

'That's a special place,' Thomas mutters. 'We should stay out.'

'Yes,' John says. 'Yes, you should. But people want things. Buildings. Cars. Bikes. Paperclips. Endless shit.'

'That we do,' Thomas agrees, crossing his arms, pensive. 'But, y'know, things can change. I remember the Franklin Dam protest—'

John and Kim moan at once: 'Please! No more about the Franklin Dam!'

Thomas chuckles, raising his arms in surrender. 'Apologies. Excuse the old fogey here.' He gets slowly and sorely to his feet, grumbling a little as he straightens his trunk. 'Told you I could get him to open up,' he says to John and Kim, motioning towards Arne. 'I'm off to bed. I trust you'll all put out the fire, proper. Total fire ban, even up here. Starting tomorrow.'

ARNE WAKES TO BURNING IN THE MORNING. After flailing around in his tiny cicada-shaped tent, he dives pantless out into the campsite, boots in hand. But their camp is fireless; he shivers, even.

The morning light, peeking through the waving gum foliage and mottling the earth, has surrendered to a great shroud, black and rising, purling high in the sky to the north and west. It is trending towards them, and on Twitter, this latter piece of information—#tassiebushfires—being shared by a rather alarmed Kim.

The professor is nowhere to be seen. On one of his dawn hikes, they presume. They try calling him. As usual, he does not answer. John suggests they go find him—and that Arne put some goddamn pants on. Arne agrees, leaping back into his tent to get dressed.

They strike out, searching along the trails that have a clear view of the bushfires rising out of the horizon. Quickly they spy Thomas standing motionless on a rocky outcrop, peering through binoculars towards the fires in the far distance, billowing and painting the vista black. John turns a palm to the sky and, to Arne's horror, captures motes of falling ash on the wind. Middens of them, piling in his hand.

The world around them burns and Thomas says nothing. Speechless, but crooning to himself, he creates an echo: *It can't burn. It can't burn. It can't burn.*

'What do you mean it can't fucking burn?' John yells.

Thomas whirls. He rushes towards his students, leaping gracefully from rock to boulder and boulder to rock. When he reaches them, he hands over a map covered in intricate red scrawls, detailed notes of flora and fauna. John holds it up for Arne and Kim to see.

'That!' Thomas exclaims, whacking his forefinger over a ring of red lassoing a vast inch of verdant land. 'That is the central plateau. Old growth—pines over a thousand years old. A World Heritage Area. It cannot burn. If they do, they won't come back. That's it! Gone!'

FOR TOO MANY DAYS that ancient pine wilderness dies. A dwindling miracle a thousand years tall and burning down. Dry lightning, striking where it never has; fire, kindling beneath as it never has. Hectares of colossi gone, never having had a need to adapt to this threat, the tablelands they root into remaining sodden for millennia until humanity began the bipedal busywork of extraction and emission.

Pencil pines, ragged and richly bogged. King Williams, clawing and spiralling to modest heights. And the bedded communities of cushion plants at the floor—on which hiking children have long bounced and bombed—amassing over the ages upon the skeletal remains of those that came before, generation after generation buttressing the next. A great green architecture, intergenerational wealth, real growth.

By the end of the month—the first of the year—almost all of that heritage is lost, burned out of existence. It will not come back.

After instructing his students to head south to Hobart and fly home to Melbourne, which they do so reluctantly, Thomas remains. He spends the days on standby, waiting from the relatively safe distance of nearby towns. He makes offices of pubs. He takes phone calls, gives interviews and waits, palliatively and patiently, to be called upon to venture up into the deadland. He would do so alone anyway, but the professional request that will invariably arrive at fire's end might lend him, he tells himself, a barrier—a layer of defence. Science will protect him from suffering.

It's a pervasive self-illusion. He knows too well how knowledge deepens loss.

THE FIRES DIE EVENTUALLY. And Thomas is, indeed, one of the several consulted high sylvan priests.

When he steps up into the place he does not want to be, struggling over a rise in the land, it appears before him as the first funeral pyre of the Earth. A portent like no other of things to come. The destruction, so total. The erasure of species once thought out of fire's range, so black and final. Another milestone of human progress: extinction.

A deep grief like ice cracking splits the part of Thomas where joy—even with all his knowledge—used to reside. That deeply physical pang, so unexpected, feels somehow inevitable now. There is nothing he can do about any of it; there is nothing he could ever have done.

Over the weeks, as he and several other experts—some ambitious and high-climbing like vines, others humble and slotted into the ground like perennials—survey the wasteland, Thomas starts to conjure the ends of things. That which is unimaginable. Oftentimes he turns to statue and stares deep into the future. Until he is nudged and returns. They all confide in one another, offering platitudes and solaces. But in the tented solitude of night, the realists among them retreat into their own inner worlds, where endings stir. And although Thomas is ashamed of it, he wants more than anything to leave this forsaken place that people will soon not be able to remember.

On the final night of this long nightmare, Thomas steps out of his tent, headlamp strapped to his aching skull, guiding him across the failing shadowland, as he makes his way to a nearby escarpment. He turns his headlamp off—he has to see it. Out over the edge of the cliff, the surviving forest of sentinels below, safe and stretching for miles, uninterrupted and illuminated by the most perfect of moons. The world of green is so full before him, lit up beneath that lunatic of a rock passing through the starriest of night skies, bewildering, punching him in the lungs. He manages a gasp. But he is caught frozen, thinking of *other* friends. Of family. Above all else, he contemplates the world to come for his students. Their children. And their children's children. Flowing out into many unimaginable futures, rushing on at an unstoppable speed, racing towards the finish line of civilisation's great take.

It's a passing moment of fellow feeling, before Thomas—the professor and confessor—tunes down to the great kingdom beyond, trying to hear things he cannot. That older order of life, down there below but in so many ways above, semaphores that moment with many billions of airborne signals. Roots log in to the world's oldest internet—a fungal network of mycelia—trading meaning down below, out of hearing's range.

They hum something his falling body can't quite grasp onto. He draws in the deepest breath and, in moonlit freefall, echoes: *I want you all to survive what is coming.*

2
CAMPUS

Carbon dioxide parts per million: 403.15

Evie Weatherall arrives in the spring. She finds a mouldy deathtrap apartment on the third floor of a collapsing building in Melbourne's inner northeast—prime real estate—where a wild array of aimless human nothings go by at the hungry speed of *everything*. Coffee and transient share-house rebellion. Deep house, sex and psychoactive workouts. Shops shovelling streetwear and kicks made by Cambodian children. Rattling trams powered by brown coal, billowing over the countryside from a soon-to-be decommissioned powerplant, one hundred and sixty-four kilometres east.

A window becomes the world. For three weeks Evie wedges herself among unpacked boxes and watches the never-ending entertainment, the precious and helpless human hive, from the vantage of a crumbling window frame. She pots green living things, jades, weeping figs and Thai basil saplings. Time turns to millimetres, the days to nothing. She crafts fantastic plots for stones, pebble people rickled together and cast apart in delicate windowsill dramas, before coming to rest around the roots of their green gods, each congregation nestled safe in its one true terracotta church.

When she ventures out, it is a brief alimentary affair. She finds a pho so hot and good that the fabric of space and time open before her, the surrounding couples gawking at this young black woman, hooting and slamming the table in basic delight. Not all eatings are so transcendent. Most food, she discovers, like the Clapham corners of London, is expensive, if not mediocre; she quickly turns to the bafflingly fresh and free nightly cornucopias of alleyway bins: capsicums, vine cherry tomatoes, chorizo, seven of the sixteen hundred varieties of French fromage, pomegranates, unsmashed avocados, Belgian cooking chocolate, endless sacks of breads. Almost as flavoursome and divine as her three years of purposeful waywardness, passing on postgrad pathways, taking vacation from vocation, alighting on branches of the globe, perching in stillness a week, a month, a season.

Getting high on local sinsemilla, plucked and ponging by a lake in Pokhara, ascending thereafter for weeks into the glorious Himalayan peaks of Annapurna and Machapuchare, the tenth and twelfth tallest of all Earthly entities; watching malaria pass down the ever-rising Mekong through post-traumatic communities; waylaying in a wildfire California for an unmemorable amount of time, the LA smog and statewide smoke amassing to one dense apocalyptic horror, from which she escaped—not before a few rides of space and splash mountains—by way of Mexico, where she was robbed, not unkindly, midway through butchering the pitiful remnants of her second-year intermediate Spanish; and finally to Jamaica for six special weeks with her grandmother, gravelling and graceful, always putting time and a washing basket aside to lambast her daughter—Evie's mother—for abandoning her the way she did and flinging her foolish self across the Atlantic to south London.

Throughout those weeks, Sheila made Evie laugh and smile more than any other human had in all her life. The woman was fierce in a way the world, her father included, told her not to be. She imbibed what little she could of her grandmother's uncontainable spirit before moving on, promising to visit again one day.

Evie was not entirely without a home in these years. Every wet season she would return from afar to the same rotting, discoloured structure in Trincomalee, Sri Lanka—secured through her old undergrad marine bio networks—the harbour of which she would bound out from at the break of each day, searching the Bay of Bengal for the great carriers of deep secrets and manifold truths.

Through the monsoon, hammering and humid, she would sit, silent and sweating, waiting to chance upon spinner dolphins, sperm whales and the biggest bodily mystery of them all: the Blue itself, breaching and revealing to Evie just how small and insignificant she was—*forget your little self.* Three seasons brought unlimited joy, but with the fourth arrived limits, dawning realities: heat she couldn't fathom, a killer monsoon and vanishing pods of ocean life. Physically, she survived.

Her burner phone boiled with frantic messages from family. She responded only to her brother, Liam. After that, her parents—her father, to be sure—politely threatened to cease financing her 'adventures' unless she returned to the logical pathways of an educated young person's life. Back to rushing through that linear maze, plotted out and certain.

And now she is here, in this cool city of progress. Where the people who lived here for tens of thousands of years are not heard. Where every few months a woman is found dead in a park. Where the homeless ever grow in number and desperation. Where things are unravelling at a speed beyond catching.

Uni starts in late summer, early next year. She'll need a job. More out of pride than necessity, as her parents' money always goes far in her frugal hands—something her father admires about her: she is no wasteful, brunching millennial, at least. He need not know about the shoplifting, hacking and rarefied haggling that enrich her daily existence. He would never understand. But her mother understands, and already knows far more than she lets on. How she misses her.

For the first time since leaving home, a feeling, foreign and belonging to someone else, sets in. Here on this lonely, large island, she wants to go home. She's embarrassed; the feeling is sinking into the wrong person. This is not her. Why now, after three years alone?

She stares at the blank, stone-white walls of her apartment for a fortnight, trying to summon meaning out of meaninglessness. Peculiar topographies rise and fall there, otherworldly indentations. An election goes by in an even stranger land, across the Pacific, that will be made great again. Summer rolls in, more brutal than in all recorded history. She realises one sweltering Thursday that somehow, inconceivably, she has not been to the beach. Her diving gear has remained stuffed away in one of the unpacked boxes, now harbouring intricate communities of bacteria. She's heard the beach here is shit, but a beach nonetheless.

For a week she commits to a regime of early rising, ironic yoga, Melbourne coffee imbued with the passing powers of enema, and tram trips to bayside beaches, each less beachy than the next. They are endless flats of beige gravel—upkept for the sole purpose of providing the exercising rich with a playground to prance upon in tightfitting microfibres—abrasive enough to double as an exfoliating scrub. She barges through the powerwalk babble of ageing mums, finding the right spots to snorkel beneath the sun. But she is looking farther out, always.

The following week—the first of December—she hires an inflatable packraft from a local couple and heads out into the bay, diving freely without oxygen for the first time in forever. She needs to train up again, restore her breath, her rhythms.

Approaching the holiday season, she starts to get there. Her times increase, her heart bursts and, whether out of fellow feeling or oxygen deprivation, she begins to feel a love for the final denizens of the soon-to-be-once-was-civilised world. It's been a while, this ache like being hooked up directly to the circuit board of humanity. It zaps right through her, embeds itself in sultry dreams, pleads its case over morning cups of coffee: *See, people aren't so bad.*

One evening she rises to the surface of the water, bundles into the packraft and, lying there, panting and gazing up at the stupid summer sky, burning with the sunset colours of every kind of berry, begins to cry. It has taken three years and a few days.

She sits up, looks around the berry-speckled bay and tries to figure out how in the world she ended up here. The city skyline in the distance, hazily pinkened with pollution. Airliners, descending and ascending, transporting improbable numbers here and there, hurling them through the thickening atmosphere at speeds so great they shrink the world. The flickering homeward glide of hundreds of car headlights along the beach road, tuning into and churning out garbage. The world at ease with this great acceleration. The whole panorama, beautiful and calm, chills her.

Finally, after many innocent years of zen, Evie wants to do something so basic as to open her mouth and talk with someone close to her about any meaningless trifle.

She runs home across the city—not before dropping the borrowed packraft off at the kind couple's house, expressing her love for them as they move to show her out the door—dripping with the salts of sweat and sea, beneath the brightening constellation Crux, which has suffered the sharp but dull fate of being inked onto the calves and shoulders of the impressionable across the continent.

She bursts into her stuffy apartment, slams the door closed behind her and rushes over to a box she has left for many months above the warped inbuilt wardrobes of her imperfect square of a bedroom. She throws it to the floor, tears away at the packing tape with her teeth, breaks in and extracts her screen-cracked iPhone, four generations ancient and yet so strangely familiar in her palm. The hours she used to spend with this thing.

Frustrated, she rummages through the remaining contents, like a surgeon feeling her way through vital organs, searching for the charge that will spark life. She plugs it in and waits. Until there is a buzz, a rumble demanding her immediate attention.

She hacks into the wifi next door, setting off a barrage of vibrations that seems to go on for hours—months upon months of messages and notifications. Thousands of missing missives, home at last in the divine circuitry of her pocket relic. It turns to magma in her hand. She places it down on the bench to cool, scrolling the liquid crystal screen of her neglected phone-self.

She cuts through the bullshit—she won't fall too far in so soon—and, after many dozens of updates and patches, she manages to open her WhatsApp chat with her brother. Sweet and wholesome Liam, the gentlest of them all. When she sees the last message she'd received from him, some eighteen months ago, guilt hot as lava flows through her:

> sounds like you're having so much fun sis! It all sounds so great. When I finish A-levels I reckon I'll do what you're doing. Or maybe after university, but then I would be pretty much copying you haha. Will you be home for Christmas?

She knows almost immediately that she did in fact read this message, moments before switching off from the world of beautifully rendered people, thumbed socialising and limitless entertainment. She scrolls down now through message after unanswered message and, as she begins to piece together the narrative of the most recent period of Liam's life—parental pressures to excel academically 'like Evie' in the final year of school, a Britain turned to hate, committed to retreating and closing itself off from the world, and something else, something far bigger, which Liam, in his own mild way, described as being 'really worried about the planet, about us' —she is left with shame and consequence.

In her absence, Liam wavered; but in her silence, he unravelled.

It's just after midday in Brixton. She tries to FaceTime her little brother, but to no avail. She tries over and over until she eventually collapses into bed, exhausted with concern, a reflex she has not forgotten, in spite of what Liam's final unanswered torrent of messages from a few weeks ago might have said.

She wakes to a programmed sequence of vibrations, the wooden rattle of the phone against her flaking bedside table inducing that conditioned, quickfire anxiety she has gone so long without.

Phones, they'll be pointless one day. To Evie, there's no doubt about
the way the world is going, but as she grasps the device grenading
there beside her and sees who is calling, she has no idea where
her own life is going. She disarms her exploding mess of a heart,
reaching out to tap Accept, hovering there in the dark like a sweet
lime beside the red cherry of Decline.

Wonders of this age—a few component sparks and infrared
miracles and a thousand days of wrongs can be made right. Within
a minute she makes him laugh, within four he makes her cry, and
they set off, travelling by words long into each other's day and night.

AN OPPRESSIVE WIND RISES through the streets of the city, dust-
ing the eyes, throats and lungs of millions with frayed pollen
and sunburnt duff. And Evie, in the throes of bodily meltdown,
journeys through that dense heat towards the campus she had no
intention of ever visiting. New Zealand, Vanuatu, Chile, wherever
else—these all seemed better places for a stormy heart's landfall
than this crazy colony.

Until now.

After she reached out to Liam, and so to the world, new things
have crept in and complicated her clear, solitary life. The pull
of people.

Evie has learned from Liam that she is not alone, that by
some miracle of human collision their cousin Wally is living in
Melbourne, not far from her shithole. Liam wasn't sure what their
big Canadian cousin was doing—some writing project, he thought.
He'd been in the city for a couple of years, perhaps.

Always the talk of the family, Wally had spent his twenties
moving from place to place, continent to continent, making a name
for himself in an infuriating array of arts: intrepid climate journalist,
occasional novelist, semi-talented lead singer in an unoriginal
but confusingly popular band, and apparently a key Twittering
voice of cultural irreverence. A troubadour leaving enough charm
in his wake for swooning communities to compose improbable

mythologies. There were subreddits dedicated to him, men's style blogs that paid homage to his brand of pansexual bravura, and exactly two mid-tier gifs repurposing his prowess in the crowded category of facial expressions. He spoke too many languages and somehow always wound up waltzing into absurdly high places.

He was a right bastard growing up—the cruellest kid in Canada. An only child adept at brutal arm twists, knuckle piledrives to the spine and ceaseless treehouse pranks each and every summer they crossed the Atlantic to visit Montreal. But as Evie rounds the final scorching block, the streets emptied of souls, she remembers how much she had adored Wally. How much she, in fact, had loved him. The big cousin she waited all year to impress, who grew ever more aloof and unreachable out there by the edge of adulthood's abyss, that precipice where children are picked off by the loaded snipes of the real world.

Evie resists the feeling, but against her will she is small again— a sad girl, several years shy of her idol. That gulf only increased with Wally's summerly exaggerations, weary with sex, drugs and shoegaze, until one year he was no longer there to ignore her.

And now she is here in this burning country, where fifteen years might as well be seconds, on the verge of entering the campus bar that might put an end to loneliness. She pushes away the teasing comfort, the hope of human connection.

Just drinks with some friends, Wally had suggested when she tentatively messaged him a few days ago. *Come hang!* That sounded just fine to her.

She steps into a courtyard of trees, several grey-green entities, braiding and breaking out from beneath the blond brickwork, in search of sunlight, air and signals. They remind Evie of home. London plane. A dirty hybrid, she knows. A guiding tree here, just for her. Their boughs extend down and shelter the tables. No one in the courtyard seems to notice the gift waving above the throng of idealism and body odour. Evie experiences the faintest quiver, the irrational pull of family, however thin the branch.

AS WALLY PRETENDS TO LISTEN TO ARNE—he's banging on again about fire weather and the climate or some shit—he thinks about the girl who gave colour to his vanilla world all those years ago. He'd heard about how she had gone off the family radar after university. Good: she was always too bright for that. No one questioned him when he did the same thing, although they would have, had they known how readily he took to decadence.

Freddie continues to entertain with his little brother, as long as he can manage. John and Kim, close together, chime in when humour calls. But Wally, distracted and morbid, drifts back through time to the girl who filled his home with what he now knows to be wonder. Her fairytale accent, the lilt of each summer's hit songs, magical mountains of novels fat with fantasy, and miniaturist spiral staircases of piled sketchbooks filling with Montreal's mundane suburban animal life—a part of the living world to which, until seeing the furry and feathered inhabitants of his hometown rendered so delicately, he had never given much thought.

Humans and their beloved horizons. Whether she meant to or not, Evie taught him how to look up and down, above and below, and into things. And yet, between absent sips of beer, he ponders how he never saw Evie for all she was. She might as well have been another nut-eating occupant of the street's maples, a drawing in waiting.

Where most memories fade with years, the ones with her in them have remained, espaliering into some kind of elusive mythology. A girl sneaking into her uncle's—his father's—study, a few years before the philosopher spattered his brains across that square room of letters; a stare that could pause the flow of time, steal it for strange, higher purposes; hands sharp with the scent of smudged graphite and cedar wood shavings; an otherworldly voice, exchanging pleasantries with critters she declared equal. She was from another dimension, an agent of empathy transported back to now and tasked with getting humanity in order.

And he remembers now, flinching a little with shame's fair flutter, how he shut her out.

A reckoning comes searing in on the air—there she is, an apparition, hovering through the crowded courtyard. He raises his hand, confessing. Sweat drips off him. She lights up and rockets to him as if he is the brightest of stars, a newly discovered inhabitable world. She lands, hugging the surface of him.

'It's so nice to see you!' she says.

'Really?'

She nods, serene and certain. 'Of course.'

Wally introduces his friends. They each introduce themselves, and in the time it takes Wally to adjust to the mythological figure beside him, pulsing with more life than he can handle, she has taken a seat at the table, sliding into keen conversation with strangers.

Wally circles, taking a place across from her. Freddie rises to buy drinks, gliding past his younger brother in an alpha dance practised throughout childhood. Sometimes Wally cannot fathom how the Bakke brothers are related, their intense love for one another being their only shared trait. *Cut from a different tree*—one of Arne's few jokes, and a dark one if you knew the Bakke brothers' runaway story. Against his own nature, Wally has grown protective of Arne, brotherly even—a foreign feeling.

A few drinks deep at the quieter end of the table, Wally and Evie flipbook through history like it was nothing and everything. She turns gravity into levity. Heavy things loft on light words. Somehow, this is worse; her kindness makes him ache. He declares that she should be angry with him, to which she shrugs.

'Why?'

Wally frowns, rueful. 'Because I was *awful*.'

She nods, her eyes holding him to account now. 'True.' She recalls the oppressive loneliness of one sad Canadian summer—the hottest on record, though not for long. 'Let's save this,' she says, placing her palms down on the table, sliding them towards him, 'for another time.'

'You're staying?' Wally exclaims, eyebrows raised.

'Yeah, why the fuck not? You?'

'Well, yeah,' he manages, surprised. 'I've got this writing thing. But Liam made it sound as though you were moving on soon.'

Evie grins. 'Changed my mind. For now.'

A sense is hovering between them of how tied to one another they truly were. And now, years later, retracing those old threads, they find nothing has come undone. It startles more than just one heart. In the dumb din of bar banter, the evening sky brushed with wild strokes of fairy floss, a slight cool change gushing in from the south—Tasmania, Antarctica—that would make even the most alarmed believe all was right in the world, they dissolve time, settling into a companionable silence mastered way back in the nesting grounds of childhood summers.

Wordless, they recognise it together.

Something close to calm descends upon Wally. As close as he'll ever get. He tries not to think about the thing they all think about—the thing he writes about each day. But he does, and, sighing, rolls one. 'You get high?'

'Only with friends,' Evie says. 'Or cousins.'

'Aren't we both?'

'Maybe,' she teases.

For the first time in as long as Wally's substance-addled brain can recall, he feels the warm glow of family, that peculiar kinfolk sense, a savannah sickness that imperils the planet. The real clan is one and greater, stretching back billions of years to a common root called *life*. He feels ill at having a thought so inane and unformulated. But loneliness does strange work. And he's been listening to Arne too much lately, who has been listening to that cantankerous supervisor of his, the one who, since surviving a fall from a cliff in Tasmania after the fires last summer, has taken on the hybrid persona of an academic guru—studiously stupid and intoxicating to far too many.

Wally lights up, emitting.

Catching the earthy stink of green, Kim and Freddie close in. Arne and John keep to the periphery, holding forth in the way only they can. Wally detects the fleeting curiosity with which Evie, mid-drag, considers his crew—distant objects from somewhere far away, vectoring in on her system. A wonderfully dubious, colourful collection of comets, he sees now; he would like to stay in their company for as long as possible.

Evie charts the flicker in her cousin's eyes, a mawkishness of which she would have once thought him incapable—but there's something else there she recognises, something broken. She asks him what he is thinking about.

He takes far too long to answer for anything he says to be true. 'Heaps of stuff, I guess.'

'That so? Broody man,' she remarks, impersonating his scowl and puffing little green dreams into the midnight air. 'Men always think their feelings are special. Unique. The centre of creation. As if they don't know where the sun is.'

'Even queers like me?' Wally asks, trying an umbrella beneath which he has never truly fitted.

'I said men, didn't I?'

He should be offended but it feels vaguely true in his case. 'Sounds like pop psychology.'

She shrugs. 'It is. I'm playing.'

'Trolling?'

'Perhaps.' A great clarity filters through Evie, the past three years of her life come into staggeringly quick focus. 'But what I really mean is: maybe we're not alone, even when we think we are.'

He looks up at her, intrigued. 'You've felt alone?'

'Of course. Particularly since arriving here. But'—she gestures down the table, nodding and tipping the joint—'you've got good people, by the looks of it. And fans—followers—from what I hear.'

The rest of the crew—Arne and John—make their way down, forming a lopsided huddle at this end of the table, their desire to group outweighing their aversion to pot.

Evie adds an eager but mocking final query: 'Any groupies?'

He sees the way the tip of her tongue is peaking through her teeth. He's happy to play along. 'A few.'

'Send them my way!' Kim leans over, cracking up, before very suddenly spinning round to Evie, switching to dead serious. 'You should see some of the guys, Eve—can I call you Eve?—crazy hot. Not as hot as my little bitch here,' she says, singling out Freddie.

Trying to keep up with the rapid pace of this woman, hair and speech streaked with electricity, Evie nods. 'Call me whatever you like.'

'So'—Kim nabs the good stuff from between Evie's fingers—'what have you and him been talking about?'

Evie looks over to her cousin, shrugging. 'Family stuff.'

'Not Wally's magnum opus?' John chimes in. The rest jump in and echo their amusement about something called *The Chronicle*.

Curious, Evie turns back to her cousin. 'No, we haven't got to whatever that is yet. That your "writing thing"?'

He nods, at ease in the corralling ring of close friends.

'Don't start on this, now, Wal!' Freddie blares, gesturing up into the great unknown—*Everything*. 'No one wants to talk about this, now of all times!' He slides right up to Evie, encroaching; she inches away, avoiding collision.

From the other end of the table, Arne sees this interaction and moves over. 'Hey, bruh, could you get another round?' Freddie— attentive, brotherly Freddie—acquiesces.

Wally sees Evie's amusement, as if this large, abrupt man were a robot masterminded by his little brother.

While Freddie stoops over the bar, forearms spread large, waiting for a slow tap's pour, laughing along with the inexperienced pourer, Arne apologises to this unfamiliar woman—Evie—for his brother. He doesn't even try to explain him.

'What's his deal?' Evie asks to no one in particular. 'He okay?'

Quiet, concealing nods, bobbing beneath her guiding trees. They embolden her. 'He always so…'

'Obnoxious?' Kim suggests. 'Yes.'

There is a hum of amused agreement from Wally, Arne and John. Elbow nudges and knowing tilts. Hard-to-catch eyerolls.

'But we're stuck with him,' John adds glibly, scratching his head, moving dark, thick tufts around. Evie likes him at once.

'Stuck loving him,' Kim adds. 'And fucking him.'

Evie senses no boast here, just a crassness more people could do with. Maybe it's the high, maybe the heat, but Kim starts to hover lightly before Evie.

Her words wobble. 'Wasn't always this way. His head has got sort of big the last few months.'

'Oh, like Wal here,' Evie cracks, prompting a round of laughter, none more genuine than from Wally himself.

They go on to explain collectively how Freddie has gone viral, a shredded poster boy for global environmental activism. He has mobilised people, garnered funding and support, and delivered far-reaching messages to media and government. But it has been a circus. Progressive yet deliciously palatable, networks—even those owned by Murdoch—have creamed at the chance to shoot him at the housewives of even the most conservative of households, regardless of what he was preaching.

'I think he'll settle down,' Kim concludes, tired but hopeful. 'Or maybe he'll just be like Wal for the rest of our days!'

'What the fuck did I do?' Wally protests, raising his hands in a fine performance of dismay. They hush down as Freddie returns with an armoury of needless drinks, which they all take up in good faith. 'What we all laughing about?'

'You, sexy Ken!' Evie bellows, raising her glass. She sees insecure vanity ringing around that beautiful noggin of his, cheeks flushed in either self-awareness or a mistaken sense of flirtation. To Evie's surprise, it turns out to be the former, as he plops himself beside his little brother and shrinks down to size.

She blows him a petite kiss, softening the blow but deepening it in many more ways.

They drink in the calm between them, silent for an unknown time. Something eases, there in the balmy dusk; Evie steps into a tribe she feels she's always known but never chanced upon. Children of the age of infinite growth, caught in that unfurling wake of great change, fuelling out into the atmosphere and oceans, rising each year, waiting to return. The slowest change in their short lives, the fastest in Earth's long reckoning.

The tribe gets to talking about the thing no one seems to talk about. Evie learns of their various stakes at the table. She's quietly kept tabs on Wally during her travels, devouring his words, making kindling of his hundreds of finished and, when rather dry, unfinished pages. And Freddie, using his large, dumb body to rail against the burning of the world. She has trouble deciphering where exactly his heart is in all this. And the three younger members—Arne, Kim, John—provide the self-conscious, clipped explanations typical of their kind. Isolated and shut off from the world, stranded on researcher island. Arne is researching something jumbled about trees and carbon cycles; Kim, greening cities with bioengineered flora; and John, something philosophical that makes her like him even more.

She's about to become one of them, she just doesn't know quite how yet. She thinks—hopes—that she and Wally can be that way together, for a while. Clueless until clues turn up.

Months back, flying along the east coast of Australia, she looked in wonder from on high at the largest living structure in the world, a pearl necklace draped across the big blue world. It calls to her still; she will go there soon.

Small and secret, she tells Wally about it, near to whispering.

'There's nothing like it,' Wally confesses. A tense moment passes between them, before he adds: 'It'll be gone soon.'

Evie knows the truth of it. *Like everything*, she thinks. Morbid. But she can't see any other way from here, as things stand, teetering on the edge for all the world to see.

Wally probes. 'Do you really want to research something that is dying?'

'Everything dies.'

'You know what I mean.'

She pauses for a while and considers it. She looks up and the trees are just trees. They give her nothing this time. She decides alone. 'Yes, I do.'

'Okay, then,' Wally says, pleased. 'We can do this together.'

Confused, she asks if he's thinking of putting in an application to the doctoral program.

'No fucking way!'

Evie clues up. 'The thing you're writing?'

'Thinking of,' he admits.

'Tell me about it.'

Wally squirms a little, and runs a hand through his ever-so-slightly thinning wild mane. Through the hazy heat, eased only a little by the cool change, more drinks arrive, courtesy of no one, it would seem—John, Wally guesses, given the silent delivery.

'Well?' Evie asks, prodding once more.

'I don't really know. Not yet.'

'You got a few years of money to write about something you haven't even figured out yet?'

Wally responds with an ambiguous head wiggle. Evie is as impressed as she is incredulous. 'Well played, cuz. Good hustle. But I shouldn't be surprised—white dudes can get anything.' Wally concedes this. 'So, what have you got so far?'

'The money or the writing?'

'The writing, you idiot! But I'll happily relieve you of some of those funds.' She looks over at the three young scholars—a doomed species she's wary of joining. 'It's harder for foreign students to get funding. Not sure I will.'

'Please, take some of mine. It's an absurd amount. And to be honest, I have no idea what I'm doing.' Wally relays how, on the eve of departing this strange land, well over a year ago now, he applied on a whim for a creative environmental writing fellowship —loosely connected to the university, but actually provided by an anonymous private donor—named after one of those German philosophers who was actually a Nazi, a detail overlooked by academia. When they offered it to him, Wally tried to turn it down. He had already arrived at the next electrifying point of his never-ending circuit—Phnom Penh. But the university, on behalf of the benefactor, upped the offer and expanded the contract to the distressingly fortunate timeframe of 'ongoing'. He could write from anywhere in the world he so pleased, but for the odd event here and there with Melbourne's moneyed elite. A few years of this and he could afford a decade of aimlessness, penning pabulum and getting high on the world before it all disappeared.

'Hah! Nice!' Evie struggles to contain her laughter. 'The *Nazi* fellowship. Place like this—of course!' They laugh at this together.

'What do they mean by *ongoing*?'

Wally looks up, gravely embarrassed. 'I mean just that. There is no end date.'

Reeling, she takes a dramatic swig of beer, acting at maintaining her balance. When she windmills the glass back down on the table, she hollers, 'What in the actual fuck! That's absurd. Did you even finish uni?'

'I did—just. BC, Vancouver. It's not really a university position —I just have a space to write here.'

'But why you? Because of the climate reporting?'

Wally raises his palms to the air, uncertain.

'Sounds like the kind of pretentious shit my father would pour money into,' Evie concludes.

'How is Uncle—'

'Don't change the subject. He's fine—the boomer wanker will always be fine. What are you writing, then?'

Wally considers pointing out that, according to Liam, Evie has been getting by largely on the generosity of her boomer wanker father, but resists. Instead, he rolls another one and considers how to convey the impossible to this cousin he once knew so well.

'I want to narrate what we're doing to the planet,' he says plainly, flattening his palms on the table.

'You want to write a novel about climate change?'

'No,' he says emphatically, throwing his hands about as if they might help him to explain. 'Something…sufficient. Record it. *Chronicle* it—a ledger, a witness statement, of sorts. For posterity. Something large. Just not sure what it is yet. Maybe I never will be.'

Evie is suddenly intent, perched and smoking and ready to arrow ideas into that part of his brain that has for months now only managed to conjure dross. She shifts a little, sober and sombre. 'That's a big ask. I don't think you can quite.'

He nods. He wants nothing more than to spend the next year writing a shitty whodunnit and thumbing tweets off to satellites up above.

'Yeah, I guess not,' he mumbles.

'What I mean is, it's all just too immense. And at a scale humans can barely comprehend. Why else haven't we done anything about it yet?'

The rest of their company look up from their ramblings, as if this were a topic for which they had a search warrant. Freddie and Kim were, until a moment ago, readying to leave. Arne and John were locked in some kind of gesticulatory warfare they seemed to be enjoying, pulling out their phones occasionally to flick things each other's way. Now they swarm.

Wally turns pensive, mulling his way towards tired defeat. 'Maybe it is all just too large—larger than us,' he says, drifting off into some horrifying place, years from here.

As quickly as Wally's friends flock to the darkness, Evie wants to drop the topic—her cousin's pained expression, frayed and greying along the waves of his hair just above the ears, prompting something inside her. A slow but powerful wave of exhaustion, complete and unrelenting, washes over her.

Closing time approaches. The stars roll across the sky, tumbling down the universe. Ancient dots break through the canopy of palmate leaves, large and lobed, all avocado and bronze in the bar's dying light. They seem to bend down in immense green handfuls, reaching out to Evie. She transfers the feeling—that new heaviness—across the table to him. The others have no idea anything is happening at all.

'Can I crash at yours?' Evie asks.

3

BLEACH

Carbon dioxide parts per million: 409.4

From the safe haven of the emptied beach, Arne watches Evie treading watchfully beneath the mangroves. She sees something and dives after it. He tracks her, following her silhouette as it glides through the clear seawater that skirts the dense and tangled maze of mangrove roots, into which she calmly enters, vanishing. An uncomfortable amount of time passes—minutes of infinity—and a sharp panic surges through Arne, numbing his extremities.

Fidgeting, he rises and legs it through the shallows, scurrying about in nervous wait, only to have her come up, as if watching for him through a periscope, from a nearby fist of roots. Laughter—a lovely laughter he can make out even while tumbling backwards through the water—takes hold of him. It trills, cracks and scatters throughout the undercurrent, rumbling low. He stays for it, drifts a lazy half-minute below, before righting himself.

Evie stands tall, her curls dripping like seaweed dangle about her, draping across the tattoos along her dark, muscular shoulders and arms. Arne tries to laugh, to feign cool, but that only makes it more awkward. She can see how unfortunately eager his care for her is becoming.

The warm wind picks up and he feels the saltwater drying on him, tight and stinging over his skin. He is growing fond of it, though, Evie and her waterworld of creeks, coastlines, reefs and open ocean, always moving, always flowing. He would like to show her the rugged, birded bushlands of inland Victoria one day, where everything seems quiet until you actually stand still and listen.

Arne ventures back in, tests the water with his toes—a reflex from living in Tasmania and Victoria most of his life. Wading clumsily toward her, he looks out beyond their boat to the majestic expanse of blue, immense beyond imagining, full of life we've barely begun to count. He is only beginning to appreciate it when it is fading from the world.

Out there, great reefs of coral are turning pale, dying in the hot sea year after year. *An underwater ossuary*, Evie's supervisor, a distinguished marine biologist, had called it.

The night before, when Evie was rummaging through the cabin to check on various pieces of equipment, the names and purposes of which Arne could not hope to identify, she explained how ocean temperatures had risen alarmingly over the past summer, meaning the corals, and the marine life that relied on them, were under threat. While changing the lens of her garishly red underwater camera, Evie sang one of her improvised tunes: *Bushfires for the birds. The ocean is burning too. Corals they are bleaching. It will all be gone soon. The fish. The whales. The sharks. It's all one big thing. They are me and you.*

Later, after dinner, they lay on the deck of the boat drinking cheap wine. Arne fell into flirting. Evie laughed him off, not unkindly, telling him he'd had one too many. But then she did something unexpected: she asked him to hold her. She rolled into his arms and, after a time, told him how when she was little—when her mother would take them on holiday back to Jamaica—she and Liam would lie on the beach at night looking up at the stars, reaching out and renaming the constellations, all with new lines and names. She then pulled Arne's arm tighter around her and asked if he would like to play this game.

Now, abuzz and lost in last night—the warmth of Evie, the moon like a grapefruit in the night sky, and the fruitless constellations he proposed and traced across the stars—he is stumbling through the shallows, stepping haphazardly around sharp clumps of coral, following her lead.

As he reaches her, he makes out something red and wimpling in the water, fibrous, like cotton being pulled apart in slow motion. Blood.

He rushes to her, but she immediately raises a hand for calm: 'Chill, Arne.'

'Are you okay?' he asks.

'I'm fine,' she says, pushing him away.

'What happened?'

'Just cut myself,' she explains, unbothered. 'On a rock.'

'Will you be alright?'

She is clearly annoyed by the question. 'Yes. Stop being dramatic. Don't go getting all chivalrous.'

Arne steps back, raising his hands.

'It's a fucking scrape,' she continues, looking directly at him now. 'It happens. I can take care of myself.'

'I know you can.'

'So act like it then. We aren't characters in some shitty movie.' She bends down, peering through the seawater to inspect the cut along her ankle. 'Just be you. I kind of like you, when you're just you.'

Without warning, Evie plunges forward and freestyles towards the boat. He dashes after her, lifting his head occasionally to admire her graceful, strong strokes. She is getting away from him. As the water gets deeper a primal panic sets in, quickening his own clumsy movements.

By the time he pulls himself up onto the hot deck, Evie is already tending to the wound, which appears to Arne horribly extensive and infectible. 'Is there anything I can do?'

'Stop asking questions,' she huffs. 'Go make something for us to eat.'

A few minutes later, he returns with some water and a few salad rolls. Evie moves to sit alone on the gunwale. She pulls her knees up to her chest, keeping her eyes on the water. So intense and determined. Vigilant. So absolutely committed to the ocean and the life it holds, right to the end. Whatever that might be. And though he feels he has committed himself to all things arboreal—has studied them deeply, looked out for them and felt a slow grief at their various and different rejuvenations and die-backs—he cannot say that he is quite like Evie. Over the past few months, since she crashed that night at his and Wally's place, he has steadily learned that nobody is.

He has sensed this many times, day after day, as they've proceeded north along enormous stretches of the Great Barrier Reef.

Arne and Evie sit in silence, feeling the slow rise and fall of the boat, watching for life. Evie has the gift of stillness, unprompted periods during which she can descend into a kind of meditative state, pulling Arne through to the other side, showing him things he completely missed before—as she does right now. Avian exchanges. The location of an incoming gust upon the surface of the water. Fish jumping. The breath of another. The more you do this, the more you see.

'Arne,' she says, startling him.

'Yes, Evie?'

'Thanks for coming with me.'

OVER THE NEXT FEW DAYS they continue their assignment. They dive down and survey the extent of the coral bleaching at designated locations. It is a eulogy in the form of data.

The nights, however, are for forgetting. They binge Netflix. They talk for hours. Laugh about nothing in particular. They get baked and lie next to each other, taking it in turns to throw a ball against the cabin roof while spouting the most ridiculous names they'll give whales when they spot them.

Tonight is different, though. Evie is serious. And sober. She is perched on her stool and glued to the receiver, waiting for acoustic signature relays from her hydrophones, the locations of which she selected based on the migration patterns of previous years. Earlier that day, another team reported seeing a pod of dwarf minkes, and another spotted a humpback whale mother and calf. Evie is waiting for their call. Epochal songs made of keening melodies and creaking percussions. 'Like Björk,' Evie states, as if that might mean something to Arne.

On his bed in the opposite corner of the cabin, Arne looks up from his sketchbook, pausing midway through a greylead rendering of a sacred kingfisher caught on camera a few days ago near Herron Island, trying to put Evie's campus lawn drawing lessons into practice, and shakes his head.

'You don't know Björk? How!' Evie blares, distracted for a minute. 'That can't be right. Like, at parties, I'm sure I've played some of her stuff.' Evie had a habit of taking over the music selection at just about any kind of gathering, usually improving the party no end. 'You'd recognise her voice if I played you some.' Evie knocks on her headphones and promises, 'I'll blast some later.'

Arne pokes fun at her absurdly large headphones. She throws a bottle of sunscreen at him and tells him that his whale listening privileges have been revoked.

'What! Why?' Arne begs, uncertain as to whether or not she is being serious.

'Because...*the patriarchy!*'

'That joke's getting old.'

'That's not your call to make.'

'I see.'

'I don't think you really do,' she says, deadpan. As ever, her mind is humming away, working on multiple levels of meaning. She could be casual and serious at once, within the same words. Infinite variations of Evie: gentle and harsh, light and dark, flaky and pensive. Arne was starting to realise these were not in fact opposites. They could be expressed and felt together. He knows he is out of his depth but cannot resist the urge to dive deeper, to see where this might go. A few nights ago, unsure of his own feelings, he texted Wally a series of long and erratic messages. Wally responded just three times:

> Leave my cousin alone, ya nose-head. Way out of your league lol

> btw I am well, glad you care so much about me.

> Gotta go on stage now buddy

Evie's expression remains unchanged as she blurts out, 'I'm fucking with you, Arne! Like I said, you're not so bad.'

'Not. So. Bad,' he repeats. 'Wait. Are you saying I do or don't get it?'

She rolls her eyes. 'I'm saying that it doesn't matter. You'll never quite get it. You can't.'

'I see...'

'But who gives a shit. We have a job to do here, and we are gonna do it well.' She unplugs the headphones and gets down from her stool, finding her balance effortlessly. She sways gracefully with the pitch and yaw of the boat, considering Arne. 'Why do you need my approval so much?' she asks.

'Because.'

'Because what?'

'I dunno...just...because I think you're great.'

She sighs deeply, looks down in disappointment. 'Don't do this.'

'Don't do what?' Arne asks.

'Arne. Listen to me carefully. I get it. I understand that we have been squashed in this boat for a couple of weeks, and your stupid penis—yes, it is stupid, they all are—has locked on to the nearest thing.'

He feels utterly called out, naked in the most profound way.

'But you need to chill out,' she continues. 'I invited you up here because we're mates. I thought I could count on you for support. Your brother's a nutjob. Kim can't swim. And Wally's... well, busy as fuck.'

'Great. Thanks,' Arne says, sullen. 'What about the other night?'

'What *about* the other night?'

'Well,' he begs, throwing hands up in frustration, as if what he was talking about were obvious.

'I wanted that in the moment,' Evie explains. 'You know it's 2017, right? Doesn't mean anything. Doesn't have to be some Hollywood bullshit. Don't be dumb. What were you thinking would happen here, anyway?'

'Nothing now, I guess.'

'Don't sulk. When your grandchildren ask you, "What was the Great Barrier Reef like?" do you really want to tell them you were too busy dicking around after some girl to take it in before it disappeared?'

'You're not just some girl.'

'You don't know me.'

'I've known you for a few months now!'

Irritated, Evie says firmly, 'You have no idea about me. Really. You don't. Trust me. There is no way *you* could possibly comprehend my shit! So don't even try to pretend to.' She is suddenly trembling, mouth closed and breathing through her nose. 'Let me make this clear for you. This work—what we are doing here—is very important to me, Arne. Very important. So help me. Don't distract me. Please.'

Arne nods slowly. 'I'll try.'

'Thank you.'

Out of nowhere, a sound comes from the receiver. A long, haunting note, followed by another a few steps lower, then an echo not so much heard as felt. Sounds far beyond hearing, scaled to a geological time signature.

Evie rushes over to the console and plugs the headphones in for higher-quality sound. She cranks the volume and encourages Arne to lean over and listen in on the can she is manipulating towards him.

The booming sound is full of eerie wonder, like nothing Arne has ever heard before, and it resounds through him. He looks over and sees how alive Evie is in this moment, relishing the elemental thrill.

'We'll have to keep an eye out for whaley boy,' she says, 'as soon as there is daylight.'

'How do you know it's a boy?'

'Because all the humpback popstars are boys. The girls don't sing, or not like this. Not like me.'

'Huh,' Arne responds, fascinated. 'How avian of them.'

'Wrong way round, mate. Life began in the ocean.'

They listen to him fade in and out for a couple of hours, falling asleep to his navigational song. When they wake in the morning, he is gone.

AS THEY SAIL INTO WARMER WATERS, further north towards Cape York, Arne increasingly comes to share Evie's sense of dread. Seeing it up close really did beckon a deeper, more visceral response. An immense loss. Perhaps this was the reason for humanity's negligible response to climate change: abstract, it could not be seen, even as such psychological distances collapsed, spilling out into the rising tide of yearly disasters.

At each of the designated locations, Evie descends. Arne often accompanies her, particularly when she is surveying the more extensive coral formations. He does this nervously—his dive training course prior to the trip was, in his view, too scant a preparation. But often she will go alone. With her every safe return Arne feels an immense relief, however fleeting. Because there is no relief. He sees the pain each time, the childlike anger she wears as she lies breathless and sprawled on the deck, defeated.

Today she goes alone, against the safety protocols of her project, though not as egregiously as when she free-dives; she is grieving. From the deck Arne looks down through the floating debris— segments of coral upended in their death—and keeps an eye on Evie's bright yellow oxygen tank as it circles around and glides over the whiteboard of bleached coral.

She is coming up now, in stages. She holds her position each metre or so, floating very still and looking down at the collapsing reef. Something is different this time. When he helps her onto the boat, he immediately sees it: something has come undone. Maybe she has finally seen too much.

Sliding her wetsuit off and throwing a flannel shirt around her shoulders, she says abruptly, 'Let's go.'

In the evening they cross paths with another boat, a team of fellow 'eyeballers' returning south after an extensive period surveying the northern reaches. The crew—two browned, middle-aged sisters and their teenage, emo-looking nephew, whose pasty skin now radiates an alarming, peeling pink—invite them to come aboard for a meal.

During dinner, the women seem keen to pass the baton. They narrate what they have seen and left behind. Great stretches of coral reduced to skeleton; invertebrate life robbed of its colour and integrity, dying slow. Some recover; others put on a spectacular display, a colourful encore as if to say thanks for nothing. Evie has watched footage of this. How the coral glows a brilliant combination of bright purple and green. This is the terminal moment, the coral deathbed. It might last a day or two, but there is no going back. One of the women deems it a kind of farewell, a resigned departure and a call to take care of others, now and into the future. Evie sees it as nothing of the sort, but keeps her opinions to herself. It is just dying. And it is ugly, even if it looks beautiful.

'And then what happens?' Arne asks, engrossed.

'What do you mean?' one of them says.

'What happens to the coral after this?'

'Well, it turns black. In time, worms and sponges invade and bore into it and tear it apart.'

See, it's just dying, Evie thinks. *And it's our fault.*

'Kinda like us,' says the boy, his voice breaking slightly. 'When we die.'

This kid gets it, Evie thinks, giving him a nod of approval.

A WEEK LATER, birds call at sunset and dolphins come sweeping along the bay in which they have laid anchor. They splash and nudge their way around the boat, dive deep beneath to mingle with one another and massacre fish. Evie sits cross-legged, looking out from the deck at the beautiful bloodshed.

She asks distantly, 'How will you do it?'

'How will I do what, Evie?'

'You know, how will you keep going...as we lose things? The world doesn't know what it's losing.'

'It's not that absolute, is it? It's not set in stone.'

'You really believe that?'

'I do. I think we can fix things.'

'You don't sound convinced.'

'Yeah, because I'm not. But that doesn't mean I don't have hope.'

Arne slides over to Evie. She leans her head on his shoulder.

They look out at the orange flakes of light playing upon the water, disappearing one by one with the sinking sun. Spouts and splashes, still visible in the waning light. Dorsal fins protruding and circling playfully around the boat. Dolphins breach the surface, their bodies shimmering in the gloaming light, then they disappear into the oncoming darkness.

AT DAWN THEY WAKE to the extraordinary sight of a great many humpback whales. They must have come in the night, the moonlight glancing off their great hides, like smooth, dark boulders ploughing in and out of the sea.

Arne brings a cup of coffee to Evie, who is still in her pyjamas, enjoying the magnificent show.

They watch as nearly a dozen robust bodies rise and fall—some over fifteen metres long, Evie loudly guesses—in striking balance. They seem to take turns performing full breaches, their dark topsides stark against the pale grey clouds hanging about. They will mate somewhere near here.

'Have you ever seen this many together?' Arne asks.

'No. These guys are from different pods, I reckon. Maybe two or three coming together here. They're happy, too—look at them playing!'

'And how—'

Evie places a finger firmly onto Arne's lips. 'Shh. Just watch.'

He does; they do.

Arne becomes caught in the rhythm of their individual and collective movement. Their great leaps. Flipper slaps—a sound like wet rubber slipping over skin—just behind him. Fluke slams creating an impossibly large splash, and another smaller one nearby, out of view.

Arne turns and catches a brief glimpse of Evie sinking below, gearless but for her bright red camera. He rushes around frantically, struggling to suit up, but then gives up—the moment is swimming away. Whirling, he springs lightly up to the edge of the deck and takes a deep breath.

4
COMMITTED

Carbon dioxide parts per million: 422.5

Arne and Evie are busy with the old work of falling in love. A love so young it hasn't the time for slowing down. The oldest song in the book of humans, burning every other page. A rapid, grabbing, snatching thing, proceeding at the pace of young yearning. Infinite, it consumes a finite world.

People will do anything for it—this thing we can't define. Love. It makes us buy things. Fly to places. Throw out stuff. Love makes the world go round while burning it to the ground. It could be our very undoing…

Arne tries to listen to Wally's gentle, recorded voice sounding through his gunky AirPods. He is certain in his honeymoon heart that love will save us all and anything is possible. He tunes back in, after skipping over the more artsy modules. Wally is now walking through the Political Events Module, of which they've all suffered many drafts. Arne pretends to understand *The Climate Chronicle*, but in truth it's beyond him. The Conference of the Parties, their failures now: Copenhagen 2009; Paris 2015; Santiago 2019, until it went up in flames, relocating to Madrid; COVID-19 and Glasgow 2021; Sharm El Sheikh 2022 and Dubai 2023.

They've committed to warming…

Arne believes he chased her here to this great big purring city, as countless men, written by men, have done for decades in endlessly terrible movies. But no—Evie decided that part for him. After many years of toing and froing, she brought him here.

But the world has shown its signs. In weather. In flood and fire. And in disease, variant after variant. And now empires topple; people take to the streets... This decade is critical...

There have been midnight stomps through streets aggrieved—some his, and some hers.

Burning memories take their toll. Of the eve of this decade. Of Mallacoota. Of the unheard sound of millions of gumleaves, crackling and descending from above, falling and folding to ash in portents more accurate than any leaf reading. Of thousands of people and animals huddled on the beach in the blood-red light, as a wall of fire approached, radiating into their flesh and bone, only to be blown away north at the last minute, misfortune rolling elsewhere.

And of their escape here just weeks later, back to Evie's home, moments before Britain went into a lockdown half-hearted enough to ensure years of untold suffering, in the interest of the greedy few.

Everywhere...

In hindsight, they should have remained in Australia; it's no longer so simple.

In the London fog, Arne ungloves his hands. He reaches out, palms upturned to catch the soft drizzle, hoping to shake away the old country burning away inside him. That suffocating blanket of smoke pulled tight to the edges of the ancient continent, season after disappearing season. Billions of gums going up like roman candles. Millions of frightened animals, singed in their run. And then the impossible scale of death stretching out into the future. The next climate extreme, the next wave of disease, the next great unrest. It goes with him—with them—wherever they go. Who could bring life into this world, at a time like now?

People are on the move, abandoned by systems... refugees of Earth.

Looking around, monitoring his distance from others, Arne unpeels his mask. Tilting his head back, he breathes in the cool air as if it were clean and clear and the world returned to normal, whatever that might be. He lets the drizzle pamper his tongue, a stranger to this wonderfully dreary isle still. And then he thinks of the temporary respite, the brief ease in emissions at the start of the decade, teasing.

We cannot wait for the uncertain promise of a post-COVID world to begin the great transitions required for our survival...a lack of political and economic willpower...If COVID was our chance at a trial run on global cooperation, to prepare us for what is happening to our planet, then we failed...

On the other side of Clapham, several blocks away, Evie pauses from running her triangular circuit of the Common. Panting through nausea, she forms a fist in the air, stopping her pods from playing back voice drafts of Wally's never-ending work of disaster art. It's coming along, but only as the world deteriorates. She tries not to think about it. She's freezing, which helps. Soon she will be able to interact with Wally's work—or so he claims.

She looks around now, sees no one. She takes a seat on a park bench—*their* bench. Sweat sets against her skin, icy. Breath clouds her view and judgement. Maybe she should apologise. Only if he does.

She swipes and rolls, playing back from the start.

They've committed to warming...

She forms a fist.

Silence. For her and the one inside her. She listens, tries to feel for it—as she might for the rest of her time. Her hands hover, so close to life, before finally settling onto it. Rounding, rising and falling, somewhere in there.

Together, eyes closed; the world calm.

The moment eventually slides away in the din of the city, where all things great and small seem harder to keep. She opens her fist.

To some degree...

She knows this bit: another sweet little human for the vanishing world.

The world can no longer carry what it is holding...

Evie brings her arms tight to her belly, pythoning around her middle and side. Warming.

They've argued every night this week and they don't even know why—they agree, after all. It makes her shudder.

Too much energy in the system...

'We're just hungry,' Evie says to herself. Not as hungry as most, but hungry, nonetheless. And tired. She's always so tired now.

She keeps an eye out for him, scanning the edge of the Common. London, despite this hellfire decade of disaster and austerity, has been kind to them in its own strange way, offering a few final years of peace, as Evie sees it. The last they might ever know. Things are coming, even if Arne cannot envision them the way she can, simmering away. For he believes as ever that the worst is now—the planet, the pandemic—when Evie knows by data and by heart that it is only just beginning.

There is a delay to such forcings. The ocean churns...

The world. The big blue thing of which she's seen too much. She knows how it fails, how it will crumble in the hands of humans, just how easily it ends.

We are playing with fire...

The lapsed doctoral student in her—just one of the many cruel consequences of long COVID—appreciates that it's more complex than that. Or is that Dr Arne Bakke, her healthy other half, speaking for her? It won't all just end in a flash. That's too easy. The struggle will go on.

Our children will live through unspeakable change...

She rubs her belly, notes a soreness she's not felt before, deep within. Out of nowhere she begins to cry, spluttering and laughing at the absurdity of it all. 'Fuck off, Wal. Christ.' She leans forward and rubs her temples.

And why? Because we can't imagine something better?

She's about to get all messy when she makes out Arne, looping through a nearby woodland, a particular spot he's drawn to,

columned and redolent of ash, lime, plane and horse chestnut,
arriving along their agreed cooling-off path. This is the place they
go when nothing else will do.

When the world is collapsing...

Evie wishes she had Arne's spring these days. In a few months,
she'll be a whale. Smiling, she makes a few cetaceous clicks with
her teeth. She's out of practice. Too much time isolating in the
studio, drawing them and not being with them. There are some
pods up in Scotland she wants to take Arne to see. Minke, mainly.
But part of her wants to leave them alone. They can't afford the
trip anyway.

Arne finally approaches, sullen; she softens and is immediately
angry with herself for doing so. She never thought she would be
so basic as to simply want them to be okay. But in the uncertainty
of everything, it is all she wants. Looking up at him, she forms a
fist. They consider each other awhile, looking away occasionally,
figuring out what to say. The wind picks up a little. Their breath
plumes in wonder between them. The night, beyond the flickering
cityscape of golds and reds, shifts down to something startlingly
dark. Stray stars break through the drizzle and things are suddenly
clear to Evie.

'What are we going to do, Arne?'

He shrugs, motioning that he might sit beside her. She pats the
spot, and then starts to trace a circle with the tips of her fingers,
warming it. He joins her; they sit in companionable silence—just
the three of them—for as long as the busy, spinning world will let
them. Many little revolutions happen there and then, their hands
searching and entwining, over and over, as time keeps running away.

'I don't know, Evie,' Arne says.

Her voice plummets down through her, lost. 'Please,' she
manages. Arne moves to comfort her, but she holds him back,
looking for clarity. 'We can't afford it. We're too young. We have
things to do. And besides...'

'What?' Arne begs.

'Look around you, Arne.' She waves her hands wearily through the air at *everything*.

He knows the thought, the feeling. 'You want to move to another planet?' he jokes.

She punches him in the arm, telling him to shut up. But she knows, even though Arne might not, that one day, not long from now, some rich arseholes will try exactly that; they'll send the poor first to die and do all the labour, and then the tech billionaires, fascist dictators and assorted elites will ship out of here. Elon Musketeers have been scrambling to prepare the groundwork. And short of that, as the world's resources shrink, they'll find ways to keep themselves safe for years to come—gated towers and domes, self-contained babels and bubbles. Clean air and drinking water for the few, a dying Earth for the many. You'll need loot and luck to get in. Her father would secure a spot, she suspects, so that he might continue with his philanthropic endeavours.

In the falling dark, her green eyes send a severe spark through him.

'You feel it too, Arne. I know.'

He has been seen—his darkest, innermost thoughts brought to the surface by one of her jolts. She brings him to focus.

He sighs. 'Well, what would you have us do? You don't have to do this.'

She rolls her eyes. 'Yes, we do.'

'What?' he begs, low and puzzling through the pieces of it all.

Evie sees him softening, his eyes melting. He wants this—he wants *them*. He never really had it, so he doesn't know how fucked family can be. He and Freddie had to run from it—Freddie hasn't stopped, if reports are to be believed. She's watched the world whittle away at him throughout these spiralling years, beneath all his dumb, smiling hope.

He looks to her through the dark. 'Why?' he whispers, trembling on the verge of fatherhood.

'Arne. This won't fix things.'

He sobers as best he can. 'I know.'

She leans over and places a hand on his cheek, running a thumb over his faint stubble. 'It will only make it harder.'

'Then why do you want this?'

Want is not the right word, she thinks. But there is some strange purpose here, something inevitable about the love below, growing within, beating in time.

She sits upright, back straight against the bench, looking out across the Common towards their apartment. The lamplights like guardians illuminate the many paths from here in gold. 'Because. They will be good,' she decides.

'How do you know?'

'I just do.'

They clasp hands in sheer terror for the future, in unending hope for life. They commit to warming.

5

BENJI

Carbon dioxide parts per million: 424.7

The puzzle is rearranging right before them.

Arne focuses on Evie, quaking and wailing a deep, drawn-out mother song, a protracted siren from the body. She pulsates with purpose, resting between contractions.

He feels something like helplessness, sees that there is no one quite like Evie. No one as powerful. No one as magnificent. She is calving life from within, guiding a naked baby out of peaceful waters and into this world and its future.

Evie looks down beneath her, through the chaos of cascading sweat, wires, needles, masks, blood and shit in the sheets, midwives' hands. 'What can you see? Can you see it?' she moans.

'Ah—'

Arne receives a firm prod in the ribs from the head midwife, Dot, a stout Yorkshire woman, the tone of her voice familiar and reassuring. Shrouded in PPE, she manages to nod at him: *Go on, you daft bugger.*

'Yes,' he tries. 'Yes, Evie!'

Evie pushes right down through her body. Soon something appears. A tuft of curly, vernix-laden hair.

'Can. You. See. It?' Evie pleads, panting between each word.

'Yes!'

'Really?' she manages, sobbing now.

'Yes. Oh my god,' Arne gasps, raising his hands up to his mouth, more overwhelmed than he ever expected to be. 'I think it has dark hair. Curly, like yours.'

'Are you crying? Arne, you bastard! You are not allowed to fucking cry. I am the only one who gets to fucking cry right now!'

Rosie shows her agreement, all the while taking Evie's hand in hers. 'Okay, love. One more push. Let's get this baby out before Christmas.'

A final push and
they wait
and wait
an age
time stops
and restarts with a cry,
a frightened, alien cry.

Arne holds the child up and brings him immediately up to Evie's chest, her skin. He searches frantically, nuzzling his way around until he attaches to her.

Watch him. How he worms his way through adoring arms to fight greedily for colostrum, for life. Breathe the child in—he smells perfect. Cover him with tears, never let him go.

The pieces fit; they have come together just so.

THOSE FIRST DAYS FORM A BLUR. The ineffable surge of new parenthood reduced to ill-equipped words. Family—Wally and Liam—visit the hospital. As the blues come to Evie, John and Kim call whenever they can, regardless of the time on the other side of the world. Freddie FaceTimes Arne, insisting on closeups of the new Bakke-Weatherall boy.

But as the days go by, the world begins to intrude—its troubles encroaching on the cocoon of family, gnawing at Arne.

6
STORM

Carbon dioxide parts per million: 427.9

Through the haze of those first sleep-deprived months, Arne and Evie fail to notice just how hot and dry the start of summer has been. Records break, again. Millions flock to yellowed parks on weekends or lunch breaks to offer their pasty flesh up to the sun, as if their solar deity might at any moment depart their world for good, as if the deadly heatwaves of recent years never happened. The Earth is just inclining as ever, within a range. But other things are at play, though London—Britain, Europe, the whole world—seems again not to have noticed.

Arne and Evie are giddy with love, tetchy with fatigue. When they should have been catching up on rest they have been staring at their boy in total adoration. Benjamin. Benji. They obsess over his tiny mannerisms, his quirks; they panic at every little cry and complaint, googling what to do; they take photos and post them for all to see. Friends elsewhere return the favour, it being that time of life, that year of their century.

Arne perches on the ledge of their apartment window holding Benji, who wriggles and kicks in his arms. Further along the ledge sits Wally, who arrived from across town unexpectedly on their doorstep a few nights ago and has made himself at home.

They look out the window, beyond the sad football pitches, at the sight of thousands of pale bodies roasting in the sun across

Clapham Common. Birds sing, bicycles whirr and ding. On the footpath a floor below, three elderly men sit on a bench fanning themselves, remembering all those they have lost in recent years, and exchanging bewildered observations of weather, quips about skin cancer and the benefits of global warming.

Arne asks Wally how long he plans to stay.

Wally leans back against the window frame and runs a hand through his wild beard. 'As long as I can,' he says.

Arne takes a moment to compute this. Even after ten years of friendship, he has never really adjusted to Wally's bluntness. The things he says. The things he does. The things he writes and sings. Evie is like this too, in her own way. Their long and deep friendship has always made sense to Arne; they are more than just cousins.

'Well—'

'Stop right there.' Wally raises a hand. 'You both need me here.'

'Is that so?'

'Yes. You feel I *should* leave because that's how you're supposed to feel, like this is your time or some shit. You and Evie, playing new parents.'

'Yes, exactly. New parents, which is what we are. We're not playing. This is our life now.'

'Uh-huh. But when I rocked up last week, you guys were barely keeping it together.'

'That's because we have a baby—that's what new parents do!'

'Sure. But look around you. Look at the place.' Arne had to admit that their apartment was spotless. 'You guys are too tired to realise it, but I've cooked breakfast, lunch and dinner just about every day. Cleaned and dried your laundry. I even paid a couple of bills. And just the other night, when you were both asleep on the couch, Benji started grizzling—I think he's teething—so I attached him to Evie and held him for a feed. She didn't even notice.'

Arne finds this hilarious. 'You serious?'

'Not gonna lie, it was gross.'

'So, basically,' Arne begins, jumping on the chance to mock

Wally, 'the brilliantly talented Walter Weatherall has settled for a job as his cousin's nanny?'

'*Manny*, thank you very much. I'm exceptional.'

'I'll just stick with nanny. Men can be nannies too.'

'No, they really can't.'

'How progressive of you.'

'Whatever,' Wally says, shrugging. 'Who would hire them? You?'

'Yes! I'm hiring *you*, it seems.'

'You couldn't afford me. This is a pro bono case. Anything for this little guy,' Wally says, gazing affectionately at Benji, babbling on his father's lap.

'Look how far you've fallen. You used to hate kids.'

'Maybe I'm softening with age.' Wally extends his arms to steal Benji, who kicks with excitement.

They fall quiet, taking in the vista. Swallows across the Common tweet out seasonal confusion. They should have migrated weeks ago to winter in the southern hemisphere—South Africa, Argentina, Australia.

Wally looks down at Benji, sniffing the top of his cradle-capped head, redolent somehow of almond and cinnamon. The boy looks up at his uncle, smiling cheekily before yanking at the buttons of Wally's shirt, finally settling on sucking them. Wally considers the child, then sighs. His shoulders drop slightly. There is a sadness in him Arne has not seen before. A frailty, perhaps. Or weariness. He is not quite sure.

'How bad is it?' Arne asks.

'Well, we're going to cross two degrees, there's no going back now—'

'No, Wal, you dickhead,' Arne moans, wincing. 'I meant the other thing.'

Wally scrunches one half of his face. 'They're outside every morning, waiting. Six months now. You would think they'd have other people to harass. Or more important things to cover.' With his free hand, he mimics a photographer snapping a picture.

Arne tries to imagine it, photographers following you everywhere. Strangers demanding endless content, grammable fodder.

'London is full of wankers like us,' Wally continues. 'The fact that they even bother, with everything that's happening to the planet, is a sure sign of the end—of how truly fucked we are. But, you know, "Don't look up!"'

Arne can only nod in agreement, catching himself before he drifts too far into the future. 'And Harry?' he asks.

Wally just shakes his head and looks down, focuses on Benji. He tries not to think of the openness, of all the different people they let into their lives—the delight and confusion it brought.

'Why didn't you tell us earlier?'

'Can we just not talk about it right now?'

'Sure.'

Benji starts to cry. He's hungry, so Arne hurries him to the bedroom, where Evie is already sitting up, waiting to feed.

She and Benji share an orbit, a circuit along which they meet to exchange a sacred tongue that Arne finds himself wishing he could speak. Their language is ancient, mammalian. Full of song and mobile stars, baby breath and cooed constellations. What could he ever offer in kind?

But there are also things within Evie—visions—he cannot see.

LATER THAT EVENING, Arne joins Wally, who whips up a curry in their cramped and rotting kitchen. They pop open some beers, go back and forth, unloading burdens: Arne's painfully tedious research on rewilding; Wally's sudden and profound inability to write his latest book or further develop *The Climate Chronicle*.

Evie hovers into the loungeroom on waves of cumin and cardamom. 'Smells great, Wal. But I'm not paying you to distract him,' she says, pointing at Arne. 'I need him to sing Benji his sleepy song.'

'Need I remind you, you guys aren't paying me at all. Tell her, Arnie,' he says, whacking Arne on the backside with a wooden spoon. 'Go on! Get singing, daddy!'

Wally and Evie wait for Arne to put Benji to sleep. When he returns, they devour the curry, rice and raita together, each occupying one of three mismatching sofas—burgundy suede, navy and mottled-grey denims, items salvaged from bulky waste collections across London's south by a torch-wielding Evie late that first year, as the city was starting to open up again. She managed somehow to furnish their entire apartment out of what the wealthy had deemed expired or unusable.

Arne—and sometimes Wally—would be dragged along to assist with these 'recon missions', as she liked to call them. Arne often protested, insisting they deserved something new, something more. From the top of a rubbish pile, Evie would cast him a fierce but playful look: *You know we don't have that kind of money, and don't be like that—don't be one of them.*

On the rare occasions they went to Evie's parents for help —generally with Liam, her shield, in tow—during those first troubled years, parading their precarious lives for amusement like a cute production put on by schoolchildren, her father would recall with great affection his own time studying in the seventies and working in the eighties, inevitably perorating about the formative value of hard work, even at a time like this. Between gulps of high-mileage wine he would gaze performatively into the distance and conclude, 'It's a great time of life. So live while you can. The world is recovering.'

But they were hungry and desperate, overwhelmed. People were still dying in great numbers.

'Enjoy this time,' he would say, 'surrounded by friends and interesting people—that's how I met your mother.'

But they felt a rising despair, a great abiding fear. They were never more drawn to one another than then. And so, inside Evie, something eventually grew.

From the loungeroom they hear Benji stirring in his cot, crammed in a corner of their bedroom. He settles himself quickly. Approaching his first birthday, Benji is one of life's sleepers, much to the relief of his parents. They return to talking freely, much as they had in their Melbourne days. Meandering, comfortable, open; ebbing and flowing between attention and inattention; offhand remarks, puns and one-liners, a game with which Arne still struggles to keep apace. They gossip. They manage to Zoom John briefly into their banter, riffing on the ceaseless content coming their generation's way: shows, books, podcasts, the current gen of games, the newest *Star Wars* series, the latest and most progressive phase of the MCU. Wally tweets pure fire at various points. Evie posts their being together to her story.

Wally busts out a Highland scotch—the only thing of real value he lugged with him across town from Islington—which Evie decides to indulge in only after running the numbers, consulting her Feed Safe app. They all move forward, sliding down onto the itchy olive carpet, crawling in on the coffee table at the centre of the room.

Closer now, the mood thickens. They turn to larger things. The acceleration of everyday life. The world, more polarised than ever, rising ever upward towards oblivion. Each violent year coming and falling like one drawn at random from some distant future. An age in which the impossible has become thinkable, one disaster after another.

It took many names. The Great Acceleration. The Anthropocene. Business as usual. The Great Reset. Post-COVID. The sixth extinction event. The new normal. All happening too fast to comprehend.

Wally seems calmly fatalistic. He wolfs down the cold remains of his curry and places the bowl on the coffee table, beside one of Evie's camera lenses. Evie thinks aloud about what Freddie and Kim would say if they were here. *You can always do more*, Freddie would say. *Try harder. Think differently. The world depends on it.* Kim might not say anything. She would more than likely spend the evening listening intently, designing solutions in her head before building them over weeks and months. Melancholy surges from Evie's conduit words, a shared recognition of just how close and tightknit they all once were, and would never be again. Freddie and Kim are out there somewhere, stirring up something big, no doubt.

Wally pours three more glasses and breaks the silence: 'To Kim and Freddie.'

They bring their glasses together and repeat it. Evie takes a small sip and pours a calculated measure into Wally's glass, demanding, 'Wal, what happened with Harry?'

She has caught him off-guard.

'Well...' Wally looks at Arne and teasingly narrows his eyes, playing the part of the betrayed. 'Nothing, really. That's the problem. He got busy. I got busy. Things happened.'

Evie scuttles crab-like across the carpet to sit alongside Wally, their backs against the foot of the sofa. She reaches for her tablet on the coffee table and starts to tap and slide her fingers in an arachnoid screen dance.

Though curious what his cousin is doing, Wally continues. 'We got better for a while. When he stayed away from California. Less attention. Less murmuring around us when we were out. But we just...I dunno.' He trails off, struggling to narrate and reconcile the recent turmoil of his life. He focuses on the camera lens at the centre of the table, which, he is certain, is starting to vibrate. Moments later it whirrs a mechanical pitch, slight and dissonant. A small light flickers within the centre of the lens. Must be the whisky, or the blues; he hasn't had a hit in days, not since arriving at their place.

Evie drops her head onto Wally's shoulder, assuring him he'll be okay, her voice soft but somehow distant, her focus shifting. Arne sees it. Inwards and outwards. That is how she works, how she creates. She is rendering something for Wally onscreen, which she had often done for Arne in the aftermath of heated debates in an attempt to give life to some ineffable feeling.

Evie lifts her eyes from her screen, slips an arm around Wally and says, 'I'm sorry. Harry was alright...for a famous dude.'

'Yeah,' Wally intones, 'he was.'

'But just so you know, you're a ten and he's an eight at best.'

Wally is mildly amused, his vanity tickled, if only for a moment.

Evie leans in to kiss her dear cousin on the cheek. 'Talk about it whenever you need. No stress. You can keep your things here in the spare room—we aren't ready to move Benji in there just yet. Stay as long as you need. We've missed you. It's nice having you here.'

Wally nods, 'Thanks, guys.'

Through the window comes the sound of a dog barking, accompanied by a triplet of car honks; they trill together on the evening air, which, though still warm, catches the first susurrations of a developing cold front.

Evie mutters something excitedly beneath her breath. She leaps to her feet to turn the lights off and quickly returns to her place next to Wally, before performing a final emphatic tap on her tablet. Stars light up in her eyes as she nods towards the table, over which fragments of light come into being, shimmering like stardust. Evie's hands conduct some final onscreen touches, like a spider assembling the final perfect lines on her web. The illuminated puzzle pieces come together in a smooth digital dance. A whale. A three-dimensional hologram of a humpback, taxonomical in outline yet ornamented with strokes and flicks of azures, pinks and lemon yellows. Evie gives the onscreen tail a little nudge, as a delighted child might a mobile, and sends the hologram into the middle of the room twirling towards its point of projection, where it comes to a halt just a few inches above the lens.

How Evie evoked the sense that the creature was content and yet lonely, neither Arne nor Wally could tell. Only she knew these tricks. It left an impression of deliberate incompletion, as if there should be more: other whales, a pod, oceanic textures, myriad sea life. Not just this solitary creature.

Delighted with her newish toy—another new medium for her to work and experiment with—she explains: 'A gift. From an admirer of my work.'

'Apple? Your father?' Wally asks.

'Shut up. A startup, actually. This is one of the prototypes.'

'It's beautiful, Evie.'

'I kinda think so too. I'm working on a few different things like this. And I'll soon be getting some larger lenses, a wider holographic range and field of projection.'

'Huh,' Wally says, impressed. He considers the piece for a moment, moving closer and running his hand through it, disrupting the form. 'I could use your help. This could get people to look up and pay attention. This could be huge.'

A FAST-MOVING DEPRESSION sweeps across the Atlantic, and within days a kingdom disunites, falling apart once more. An extreme weather event in every sense, even by recent standards. Unfathomable winds and rains, storm damage and flash flooding, spectacular to the degree that it was also unimaginable. It defies logic, experience, weather itself.

When the first warnings came from authorities, armchair experts collectively sold a wide range of visions. Amid this circus, one actual expert—an exasperated Scottish meteorologist more concerned with providing clear and accurate information than with being derailed by the denialist ploys of popular media—let slip that this would be a 'real super-fuck-storm'; the clip went viral and ascended forever into the memosphere. People worked like mad to deliver their KPIs before the weekend real super-fuck-storm, their bosses meanwhile escaping north to various country properties sometime during the middle of that Friday, lining one side of the M1 with Jaguars, Bentleys and Aston-Martins.

It arrived ahead of schedule, late in the afternoon, to render the city unpassable, leaving people stranded and families riven. And how quickly things descended in the metropolis—transport, hospitals, communications, sewerage, gas, power. They all seemed to bow to an elemental command. Some withstood the onslaught longer, stayed the course—hospitals and emergency services, on the back of individual sacrifices and collective perseverance, a resigned workforce inured to large-scale crises and decades of murderous governance. But eventually things fell apart.

THEY ARE STILL FALLING APART as Wally and Arne wade through the floodwater. The air is quiet, eerily so, but it is welcome after nearly forty-eight hours of onslaught. Arne starts to shiver. Wally notices and moves to bring him into his body, beneath his coat. They trudge across the Common, turned now to marsh. Arne suggests the cold is good, that there will be less disease. He is in shock. Others should concern them, Wally thinks. If things don't improve, if the water does not recede quickly and that state called normality resume, there will be violence and police brutality.

In the crowded greyness people scurry about like water rats, raising phones to the sky in hope of some signal, some calling. They sing out the names of loved ones, searching. An old lady stoops in the water, ailing but unaided.

'We need to find Evie and Benji,' Arne gasps, the panic rising in his throat like a snake.

They keep moving forward.

Arne does not look back.

CENTURY'S MIDDLE

7

ADRIFT

Carbon dioxide parts per million: 548.6

Evie drifts alone.

Six weeks she has spent now in the stuffy cabin of this flat-bottomed aluminium boat, waiting for migrating whales to pass through on their way to safe breeding grounds. The air is unbearable, a hot and thick blanket difficult to breathe beneath. She wards off sleep, keeps a steady eye on the bobbing horizon, out of which an immense dark force is rising like a primeval creature scaling the edge of the world. Although the storm is forecast to pass safely to the east, the sight of it and the crackling sound booming around the bay pull some inner strings within her to an unbearable tension, every muscle and sinew tightening over her bones.

She thought she would find something here. But there is only loneliness and far too much time. London, over and over in her mind and forgotten, buried. The flood and the fall.

The manifold fates and destinies, the close calls and unbearable misfortunes cast indifferently across the city. It recovered, rebuilt and redesigned, taking its cue from other cities that had dealt with similar disasters. The true damage lay elsewhere, within. And her own place in this nexus—what might and might not have been—has eaten away at her all these years, shucked every inch of her until there remained only an empty shell.

Grief. It takes hold of her in flashing paroxysms: what could she have done differently? What could Arne or Wally have done?

She is haunted by another Evie, a fuller, happier Evie, who is out there somewhere in a time and place where things turned out otherwise. Some vital detail, different: a simple choice, a direction walked, a swifter decision made, a louder scream in the hospital.

She takes her meds, struggles to keep the acrid capsules down as the cabin rocks about aimlessly, pitching and rolling with the motion of the sea. She lies down on the inflatable mattress, damp with sweat. She looks at her wrist: heartrate dropping.

She is descending now, diving deeper and deeper below. In these dreams a white figure floats before her. It is this other Evie.

What's my boy like? Evie will ask.

He's beautiful. Brilliant.

What does he like?

Music.

Are you taking good care of him?

Yes, of course.

Good, our Evie will say, composed.

What is that pill you just took?

Nothing. Just something I take.

What for?

You know what for.

Yes, I suppose so. There are others, other children you need to be there for. I can't see them from here. What are their names again? I forget. These visits fade in the day.

Raphael and Jasmine. Raph and Jazz.

What are they like?

They're wonderful.

I'd like to know more about—

A loud blare like a foghorn draws her up to the waking surface. She sits up, breathing heavily. She spots her lenses, resting besides the fathometer atop the navigational desk, sounding off Raph's tone. She leaps across the cabin and puts them on.

There he is. Raph's semblance, full of digital depth and detail, his chunky voice conducted through the bones of her skull by transducers along the arms of her frames, leaving her ears free to listen out for any cetaceous chatter on the acoustic monitoring console. The bone conduction always tickles at first, although not as much as a couple years ago when she was still integrating, when she first started bifurcating, casting herself here and there. Always home, always away; wherever she was, she could be elsewhere.

She throws herself back onto the dank mattress, slides an arm up behind her neck and cushions the back of her head, beaming. 'Hi, sweetheart!'

'Hi, Mum.'

'How are you?'

'Fine.'

'That's good. You behaving yourself? Being a good big brother?'

'Yesss, Mum.'

'What's up, sweetie?'

'Is the big storm going to get you?'

'No, it's a long way from here.'

'That's what Dad said.'

'Well, he's right.'

'Said it would hit lots of small islands.'

'Yes, but you don't have to worry about that.'

'Are there people on those small islands?'

'Well, yes.'

'Will anybody help them?'

'Yes, of course they will.'

'Will you?'

'I can't right now.'

'How come?'

'I just can't right now.'

'But who will help them?'

'Sweetie, you're getting worked up. There are people who will help them, I'm sure. Now, are you helping take care of Jazziepants?'

'I said yesss. But she's so annoying. She plays with all my stuff.'

'Well, you'll just have to teach her how to share.'

'Aren't you and Dad supposed to do that?'

'Yes, but big brothers can do that too. She adores you, Raph. That's why she wants to play with your things—because they're yours.'

'Kay.'

Evie sits up and looks through Raph's silhouette out the cabin window. The day is disappearing. Thin strokes of sunlight break through the clouds, brushing the bay gold. She steps out onto the deck for a clearer view, telling Raph to sync to her camera so she can share the view. He does so, disappearing from her lenses in the process. She shudders—the air is cooler now. They look out together, continuing.

'How's school?'

'Good.'

'Learn anything new today?'

'Umm, nope.'

'What! Nothing?'

'Mum, when are you coming home?'

'I'm with you now, aren't I?'

'Sort of. But I mean, like, when will you be *home* home?'

'Not sure exactly. I just have a bit more work to do here, then I can come home.'

'Have you seen anything cool yet?'

'Well, there's this sunset. That cool enough for you?'

'I guess so. But I meant like animals.'

'Okay…well, I saw some seals last week. A pod of dolphins a couple of nights ago.'

'So no sharks?'

'No sharks. Nobody sees them, really.'

'Good. Because they would eat you.'

'Only if they were hungry. And if there was nothing better to eat.'

'Like fish?'

'Yes, like fish.'

'Like yummy tunaaaaa!'

'Has Dad been spoiling you with that stuff?'

'Oh. Um. Nope. No, he hasn't.'

'Sure.'

'Mum, he hasn't!'

'Whatever you say.'

'It was just once.'

'Relax, it's okay.' Evie leaps back down below into the cabin. She turns off her camera, resurrecting Raph's semblance in the process.

'Hey! I can't see anything!'

'Look at Mummy instead!'

'Fine.'

'Sorry, sweetie, it's just getting dark. And I'd like to talk face-to-face a little longer.'

She looks out again and scans the surface. The ocean plays its usual tricks in the fading light—a whitecap, a protruding section of rock teasingly poking up like a dorsal fin. So much life below, waiting for us to look away so that it might come up to play in peace. And this is just the upper regions—the epipelagial and the mesopelagial—not the abyssal and benthic depths. Through the unthinkable extinctions and projections, Evie takes some solace in how the ocean—the great blue bed of the Earth from which life awoke—secretes away much of its treasures deep down, safe from our dangerous knowledge. Beyond our colonising reach. Beyond our view and understanding, forever. A utopia, an unseeable no-place.

'What else has been happening, Raph?'

'Umm…Uncle Wally was on the news. He got given a big prize.'

'I heard.'

'Dad says he won it for writing a book.'

'Yes, that's right.'

'I thought he wrote songs.'

'He does a lot of things.'

'Is he clever?'

'He thinks he is.'

'Oh.'

'It's a joke, Raph.'

'So, could I do that?'

'Do what?'

'Win a prize.'

'Why do you want to win a prize so much, sweetie?'

'I dunno. It'd just be cool, and you'd be proud, right, Mum?'

'I would be *so* proud!'

'So I can do it?'

'You can do whatever you like.'

'Stay up late?'

'Stop being sneaky. I meant you can be whatever you want to be.'

'But you sai—'

'Raph, quit it.'

'Fine! What about whales? Seen any?'

'No whales. But they'll be here soon.'

'I want to see one.'

'Me too, Raph, me too.'

'What makes you think you'll see one?'

'Mummy's done a lot of work, Raph. It's like a puzzle, and I think I've solved it, put it together. So I'll know right where they'll be and when.'

'Cooool! Get pictures.'

'Don't worry, I will.'

'And get some new whale songs. We're sick of the old ones.'

'Haha, okay! That isn't so easy.'

'I gotta go now. Dad says it's dinnertime. Oh, and Dad says that he and Jazz will call you tomorrow just before her bedtime.'

'Okay, sweetie. Thanks for calling. Miss you.'

'Miss you too.'

They blow kisses. He disappears, disintegrating pixel by pixel. A child vanishing. It unsettles her, unspools that which she keeps wound tight every day. The dark flood rises.

How she waded through that floodscape. Cars set adrift, sweeping up people into inescapable whirlpools and currents; trees felled by elemental forces and sent rolling downstream through the streets of London; the rippling undertow tugging at her feet, hauling her as she fought to keep Benji above the water; and then, as she turned in the direction of the Thames, an even greater surge—a wall of water.

She stumbled, tripped on something like a rubber tyre, and fell. In that moment, a flashing fear: Benji's tiny body sinking and vanishing, moving through the cold rapids.

No. She would not let him go.

She fought. She rose out of the water, spluttering and furious, with her baby held tight to her chest. Adrenalised, she charged through the swelling, looking for higher ground. Her legs buckled, giving way at the last moment as she plunged desperately into the glass siding of a bus stop, cracking multiple ribs as she protected Benji from the blow. The increasing force of the flood, now well above knee height, pinned her back against the glass siding.

She saw it coming, felt a primal rush in her blood as she looked at the inbound wall of brownish water, deafening and indifferent. She breathed a moment, squatted to brace herself. She raised Benji to the heavens and slid him on to the awning of the bus stop. He screamed and kicked there, crying out 'Mumma' at regular intervals. Evie set herself to climb, using the bin beside the bus stop to pivot off and leap up to join Benji, safe above the chaos. Once there, she did what mothers have done since the beginning of time, since before we were human, and sang to him, low and sweet through the howling wind and rain. He settled. Seconds later the floodwater came surging through, arriving with a timpani-like bang. It took everything with it. She was sure the structure would not hold. But it did.

Perched there, exposed but safe for the time being, Evie breathed deep with painful relief, inspecting Benji. Cuddling him. Kissing him. Through the storm, he cooed songlike for her, delighted with his mother.

Many hours later, once the world had stilled, they were rescued by kayak from their makeshift nest. Through it all, Benji remained with her, still breathing.

She never let him go.

EVIE WAKES IN TERROR, sitting bolt upright. She pats herself down before running two fingers compulsively along the five inches of scar tissue at her lower abdomen—Jasmine's portal to this world. Her clothes are drenched. She focuses on the gentle motion of the boat and waits for her heartrate to steady.

It is dawn. Outside, she can hear the dull clank of the anchor against the hull. Pacific gulls squawk as they land on a rocky reef farther out. She looks out to sea. The black clouds have passed. She will wait here for them. They will arrive in great numbers this year, humpbacks and southern rights. She is sure of it.

8

THE PIER

Carbon dioxide parts per million: 566.7

Above them, gulls circle on the cool breeze. They wind their way down, parachuting their wings and extending webbed feet to land on the handrail of the pier, their shadows long in the low morning sun. Beyond them, great container ships decorate the bay, nearby and far to the horizon.

Jasmine reaches out and wraps her hand around her father's middle and index finger, snapping him out of a daydream. Arne looks down and marvels at his daughter, the way her dark curls dance in the wind and flutter across her freckles. She is catching her breath after hopping the entire length of the pier, stomping along the planks and whipping up the dank smell of rotting wood to collide with the salt and rust on the air.

As they approach the end of the pier, Jasmine settles into a tired, light bounce from the toes. Arne sees how she mirrors the rhythm of the waves. Up and down, up and down. A curious creature, so strange, yet so utterly his own. But restless, like her mother. Those same otherworldly green eyes flickering about in constant thought. She looks up and says, 'Tell me more, Dad.'

'More of what, sweetie?' Arne responds.

'Things that are gone.'

'Oh, you mean like last time,' he says, nodding.

'Yeah. I liked that.'

'Why?'

'Because it was interesting. It was funny.'

'What was so funny about it?'

She scrunches up her face. 'I dunno. It was just so weird, like a story in a book.'

'Well, it sort of is a story.'

She looks up at him, seeming to understand what he means.

A schooner tacks before them, no more than fifty metres from the end of the pier, its dark solarsails cambering greedily to harness the wind and swallow the sun.

'Remind me,' Arne continues. 'What did I tell you about, last time?'

Jasmine recalls their conversation a month earlier and starts yelping. 'Rhinos!'

'Ah, right. Of course. Yes, we had rhinos. Though I only saw them in zoos.'

'And bees!'

'Did I say that?'

She nods. 'You said they disappeared.'

'Well, that's mostly true. They almost all did, for a while. But then some came back.'

'Why did they come back?'

'Because people needed them.'

'That's nice. I like that. How did they come back?'

'Well,' Arne begins, searching for the right words, 'some clever people brought them back.'

'Oh. They didn't come back all by themselves?'

Arne shakes his head. 'Not exactly.' He is sad he cannot tell her a better story, a finely etched myth, ordered and meaningful.

'If the clever people can bring back bees, then they can bring back rhinos too, right?'

'Sure, sweetie, why not,' Arne says, pulling Jasmine towards him and wrapping her in his arms.

'So, there are still bees?' she double-checks, looking intensely at her father.

'There are still bees,' he assures her.

'I'd like to see one, one day.'

'You will.' Arne squeezes her even tighter and then releases her. 'Now, what else did I say last time?'

'Um…phones!'

'But we still have phones.'

'Yes, but you said you had these ones that broke. Like, all the time.'

'Yeah. Smartphones. The first smartphones—they had screens made of glass that would break if you dropped them. Not like the stuff we have now.'

'That's silly!' she squeals.

Arne sees her imagining how things were, trying to reconstruct the quaint and simple past out of broken fragments.

'Tell me more things that are gone, Dad.'

But there are too many.

It has been over a decade since Arne and Evie fled London to start over again back in Melbourne, exchanging the city of unknowable heartbreak for the one that nearly burnt them to death, many little lives ago. But there was the flame of hope here too, a shared sense fuelled more by nostalgia than farsightedness, the city sinking into Port Phillip Bay millimetre by millimetre. Things got better for them. For a time. They had Raphael. Then Jasmine. And with them, something like joy.

It was around the time Jasmine started toddling that Arne began to notice the signs that Evie was again descending, but far deeper this time. He was descending too. Always had been, perhaps. In truth, he knew he had wandered numbly through those years a ghost, present only when throwing himself headlong into being a father. That was how he endured.

For years Arne encouraged Evie to go back to work, to return to the field—or, if not that, to her art. Something. Anything. But she rejected the notion; she needed to stay home and watch over her children.

But one day, after years of persevering, she found she could no longer continue. She could not get out of bed. Could not speak. And Arne, who had been preparing for something like this for years, seeing its portents in the snaps of domestic moments, knelt beside her, brushed her dark mane behind her ears and told her, not without some relief, that he understood: she had to get back to the sea. They needed time apart, reminding each other so irretrievably of Benji as they did.

And so Evie let go and drifted.

This might be the reason, Arne now ponders, that Jasmine always chooses, among the many other proposed family activities, to come to the beach on their Sundays, to connect to her mother in some way. Would Jasmine opt for parks or botanical gardens when he's away, he wonders, climbing through the remaining forests of the Earth when Evie is home?

He is just listing things now, forgettable objects. Credit cards. Plastic bags. Disposable coffee cups. Remote controls.

'No! I mean *real* things,' Jasmine exclaims, impatient to absorb more of the past.

'Real things?' Arne ponders.

'Yeah, like animals. People. Places.'

'Why do you want to hear about that kind of stuff?'

'Because I *like* them.'

Good answer, Arne thinks, looking down and dragging the toe of his shoe along the woodgrain of the planks, their cracks revealing the slosh of jade seawater shifting with each tidal motion, eternally renewed.

'Orangutans,' Arne suggests. 'Have I ever told you about orangutans?'

'Nope. But I know what they are.'

'Of course you do.'

'Of course I do what?' Jasmine says, peeved.

'Know. You seem to know all about everything these days.'

'What d'ya mean!' she protests. 'I've seen them in a documentary!

With that old dead guy who sounds like Granddad. The one you
and Mum love.'

'Never mind. I was just kidding.'

Arne notices the schooner lobbing off the waves, heading south
now into the body of the bay, fading rapidly into the distance.

'Did you ever see them?' Jasmine asks.

Arne nods, remembering.

'In the wild?'

'Yes, pretty much. Your mother and I were lucky enough to
see them—from a distance—in Borneo, before we had you lot.
An old friend was there.'

'What were they doing there?'

'They were trying to save them.'

'But they didn't.'

'No, they didn't.'

'But they tried.'

'Yes, they definitely tried.'

'But not hard enough.'

'What do you mean?' Arne asks, taken aback.

'Well, they're gone. And they were trying to stop that from
happening. So they tried, but just not hard enough. That's what
enough means. Enough would have saved them.'

She says this all so matter-of-factly, like an equation solved
aloud, that Arne cannot help but both admire and fear her con-
viction, so fierce and clear, unblemished by time, full of life—just
like her mother, really. He grows sad at the thought that Jasmine
could become anything other than this, that the collapsing world
would reduce her, if not endanger her.

'Was this before Benji?' Jasmine asks, as sudden as lightning.

The sound of his name, so strange in her mouth, draws something out of Arne, like a bucket dunked into a well: the name of
his firstborn son, drawn up through his chest and into the front
of his mind.

'My *bigger* brother. Was this before him?'

Arne manages to give her a tight nod.

'What happened to him?'

'You know what happened, Jazz.'

'Yeah, but I want to know more. Raph knows more than me. He said he drowned. Before we were born. But I knew that anyway. Raph says he knows other stuff but that he can't tell me about it.' Jasmine moves closer to her father and places her hand in his. 'Tell me, Dad. Please. It will be okay. I promise.'

Arne takes a deep breath and considers his daughter, this infinitely sensitive child, so attuned to the inner worlds of others. It fills him with guilt the speed at which she has had to grow up.

'He didn't drown, Jazz,' Arne begins. 'Not the way you mean.'

'So what happened?'

He asks himself the same thing every day as he wakes from worlds where everything is in its right place, where everything is as it should be.

'He drowned later. When we finally got him to the hospital. He—and your mum—had taken in a lot of water.'

'What do you mean?'

'It's called dry drowning. Happens sometimes.'

'How?' Jasmine asks, visibly disturbed.

'It just does.'

'I don't get it.'

'No. Me neither,' Arne manages. He rubs Jasmine's back absent-mindedly, staring into the distance, towards St Kilda Pier and the breakwater where families of little penguins used to nest.

'So you're saying that at the hospital they couldn't do anything?'

'No, they…'

Arne can only recall bits of that night. The chaos as they entered the emergency department, flooded in every way. Swamped. Inundated. Overwhelmed. The injured strewn about the place. Nurses and doctors sploshing about the wet floors frantically; lights flickering; parents comforting crying children; a soul-shattering howl down a corridor, followed by a faint whimper. Benji had to wait to be seen.

In Arne's mind he and Evie are always in emergency, waiting. Benji will be seen shortly; everything will be fine.

'But Mum *saved* him,' Jasmine says. 'She climbed on top of something with him, like a superhero. Like Captain Marvel. Raph said so.'

'She never let him go.' *They never will.*

Jasmine tugs at her father's shirt, forcing him to squat down to her height. His knees creak. She leans in and gives him a kiss on the cheek, catching salt. She then looks directly at him. 'Sorry, Dad. I didn't mean to upset you.'

Arne waves it off. 'That's okay, possum. It's just…I try my hardest for you. You and Raph. You know that, right? So does your mum.'

Jasmine gives him a firm, certain nod. 'You know what I think?'

'What do you think?'

'I think Mum tried hard enough.'

Arne smiles at this, only for a moment. 'Me too, Jazz. I think she tried hard enough too.'

'Can we go for a swim now?' Jasmine asks.

'Sure. That would be nice.'

WHEN THEY COME BACK IN from the water the beach is empty, left to them alone. The sand, though warm, bothers Arne. He swears it used to be finer, delicate and sparkling white underfoot. It is coarser these days, he's certain. Manmade and redeposited, a necessary adaptation after the bay was further dredged to allow the passage of a new, larger class of container ships. There is predictable outcry each time a superstorm seizes the bay and floods the beachside suburbs, where affluent homes are likely furnished with items shipped by those very containers in the first place.

They sit down on the sand. Jasmine starts to shiver.

Arne pulls a towel out from their beach bag and throws it around her. 'You okay?'

'Yep.'

'Eat something, Jazzy,' he insists, handing her a sandwich from the bag. She takes it greedily, wolfing it down.

After a while, she says, 'Dad, you're not a very good swimmer.'

He's amused. 'I know.'

'Like, you're okay. But you're not as good as me.'

'That's true,' Arne admits, playing along. 'You're a fish. Actually, more like a dolphin. The way you move.'

'Yep. That's me,' she chimes, satisfied.

'I'm not like your mother,' Arne starts, wary.

Jasmine does not respond. She just focuses on the sand, which she is collecting now in handfuls, sifting it through her fingers. She repeats the process once. And then again. And then again. Over and over, until Arne explains.

'What I mean is I can't swim like her.'

Jasmine extends her arm out and releases a handful of sand abruptly. 'I know!'

'What's wrong?'

'Nothing.'

'You sure?'

'Yes. Stop it.'

'Stop what?'

'Worrying about me. That's all you do lately.'

'I'll always worry about you, Jazz,' Arne tries to explain. 'It's my job to worry about you. I like worrying about you—it's what I do.'

Jasmine seems bothered by this. 'But I want you to be happy.'

'But I am happy.'

'Really?'

Arne considers his daughter a moment, then reaches out and strokes her hair. 'That's not for you to worry about, okay?'

'Why not?'

'It just isn't.'

He looks back at their car, parked along the beach road. Beyond it, an ever-expanding city—a scape of looming giants, loping towards the sea, drawing closer with each passing year. They creep inland, too. They are everywhere. The city knows no bounds. One day there will be only the sea and these drowning towers. Like something out of one of Wally's dystopias.

'Dad, how come Raph doesn't come with us anymore?'

Arne shrugs. 'I'm not sure.' But he has his suspicions: how Raph has been disappearing of late, online and anonymous. Other parents were concerned too. All their kids, unmonitored and operating in a way none of them could ever quite grasp, at speeds with which they could never keep up.

'Mum would know,' Jasmine concludes.

'You're probably right.'

They take a moment to look out across the water. They breathe together. Their minds both linger on the same person they miss.

'Where is she?'

Arne gives it some thought, then points to their left, eastwards down the beach. 'That way.'

'How far?'

'I'm not sure where she is exactly. Thousands of kilometres away, though.'

Jazz bounces excitedly, the way she does when she is making up a game. 'Could we swim to her?'

'You could. But I couldn't. You're the fish.'

'What about in the packraft?'

'Sure, if you'll have me aboard.'

'I think we can fit you in. But don't eat all the food,' she says, poking him in the belly.

'Okay, okay,' Arne protests. 'I'll go get the raft out of the car and we'll go muck about, alright?'

'Sounds good.'

At the car he opens the boot. It is hot to the touch. He starts unravelling a heap of wetsuits, oars and flippers, then hauls the uninflated raft onto the footpath. He looks back along the beach and his gaze falls on his daughter. In a rush she seems so small. Infinitely so. A dark, shrinking dot in a wad of beige. Is there anything so small in this world as her?

It all comes to him in reverse: she is in Grade Two, singing some muffled song through a face mask on her way to school; she is in her first year of school, with grazed knees; she is four years old and scared of the virtual insects Raph augments around her room; she is toddling about, trying to find her muslin blanket somewhere in the depths of the couch; one special day, she is turning two, and is hysterical with laughter, blowing out twin candles and burying her fists deep beneath the mud of a chocolate cake; she is just a baby, trying to stand; she is born and smells perfect.

OUT ON THE WATER, Arne is battered by waves of mourning. Flashes in the heart, the truest glimpses of the world, unlocked from the safety of denial. His eight-year-old beside him, oar in hand, falling on the rising sea, eyeing that distant line that separates the heavens and earth, innocently aware of the fact of the future. She knows no other world, no other way forward. This is what her generation has inherited. Arne will, in the speck of time that is his distant future, recall these as the final days when colour still survived between raging summers, when the Long Heat had not yet taken hold.

Jasmine nudges him with her oar, urging him to look back to shore, where two loosely clad men stand, waving to them. 'Who's that?' she asks.

'Oh, that's Uncle Wally,' Arne mumbles. He was not expecting him to be in town for another few days.

'I know that! Who's the tall guy next to him?'

Arne mouths just the shape of his name—*Freddie*.

THEY CLINK BOTTLES, mucking about where the sea laps up the gritty sand. They watch Jasmine as she carelessly floats about in the calming sea, which glistens red and gold as the sun sets on the bruised horizon. Freddie drops down to the sand, raising his knees to his chest, resting his forearms casually, swilling his beer around. It's good stuff, not piss—hard to come by in water-poor zones. Either Freddie stole these or Wally procured them somehow. Arne dares not ask which as he squats beside his big brother in the sand, kids once more. Wally, older and aching, follows suit.

They sit in peace, watching the future splash about before them. Jasmine seems so free to them, unburdened. People pass by, the odd one performing a double-take, wriggling in vague recognition of Wally Weatherall slumped on their sinking beach. Arne sees how at ease he is with their distant but all-too-near googling.

Freddie breaks the long silence. 'You don't mind her going in like that?'

'What can I do?' Arne replies.

'Keep her safe.'

Arne turns to his brother, ready to fume. 'I *am*. Today is clean.'

'Not like it used to be,' Freddie says, sipping his beer and flicking his shades over his mane, which is thinning but somehow more glorious than ever. Behind Freddie, Wally falls backwards onto the sand and props himself up on his elbows, swigging every so often. His eyes are elsewhere, but his ears are here— a trick of his trade.

'Yeah, well, there's nothing I can do about that,' Arne claims.

'Yes, there is. Come with me. Kim misses you. I'll keep you all safe. Evie too. And you can make a difference.'

'I make a difference,' Arne snaps, looking Freddie directly in the eye.

'What, recording the decline of trees? You're a mortician.'

Arne waves him away, turning to the distance and *seeing* the world—not as it was, but as it is. And then as it could be. It overwhelms him and he rises to his feet, marching towards the water and beckoning Jasmine to come in.

She refuses. 'It's so clear today,' she declares. 'Just a few more minutes!'

Arne walks back and looks over to Wally. 'This why you brought him here? To tell me everything I'm doing wrong?'

Wally raises his hands in defence. 'No. We just happened to both be in town at the same time. We came knocking. Raph told us you'd be here.'

Arne whirls, looking down at his brother and pointing the tip of his beer bottle at him. 'Stay away from my son. Don't go putting any ideas in his head.'

Freddie takes a moment to let everyone breathe. 'Others are already doing that.'

'What the fuck's that supposed to mean?'

'You need to get him off those boards. Your son—my nephew—is becoming a little Nazi.'

'You've been spying on us?'

'I've been *looking out* for you.'

They're about to go at it when Wally rises to dive in between them. Old friends, wrestling in the sand like kids.

A sweet voice comes from behind them. 'What's going on?'

They snap out of it and start brushing sand off one another, which strikes Jasmine as both cute and hilarious. 'So where have you been?' she demands of Freddie, whose sand-dusted hair now hangs messily.

Approving of her directness, he tries to explain. 'I've been busy.'

'Really?' she says, unconvinced. 'All this time?'

Freddie sweeps his hair back into place and rises to his feet. 'Yeah, kid.'

'I'm not a kid.'

'Oh, I know. You're a smart one,' Freddie says, cocking his head, eyes twinkling, his whole being softening in a way Arne thought him incapable of. The next thing he says, though, comes as an even greater surprise.

'You know,' he begins croakily, 'one of my biggest regrets is not being around to see you more.' He moves towards her and kneels all the long way down to her level and whispers huskily, 'I'm sorry, Jazz.'

Her hair whips in the breeze, forming dark tendrils that reach out and brush him, running along his arm.

'I haven't seen you since you were about this old,' he says, raising his hand to about the height of a four-year-old. 'I've missed you. If I could have been here, I would have. And though you might not know it, everything I've done...everything I do, I do it for you.'

'For me?' she says, childlike for once.

'That's right, ki—sorry, *Jazz*.'

'You can call me kid, Uncle Freddie. I don't mind.'

Uncle. The sound of it sends a flame through him. Arne looks over and sees Freddie in a different, sunsetting light. He's old and tired and, if Arne were to guess, suffering through the middle portion of his life.

Jazz and Freddie are talking to one another in hushed tones now, and Arne tunes out, leaving them to bond. He rolls his head onto Wally's shoulder. 'Good to see you, Wal.'

Wally cracks up, turning giddy in the company of his favourite person. 'You too, Arnie. C'mon, let's go for a stroll.' Arne looks briefly to his brother and daughter, before relenting. Wally pulls him up and retrieves another two bottles from a hemp net bag, and they set off along the beach towards the pier.

The sun sinks on the world, and in the dying light Wally wraps his arm around Arne.

'*The Chron* is happening,' Wally announces, clearly nervous as they reach the underworld of the pier. They lean against the collapsing wooden posts. The tide sweeping in beneath sifts through their feet as Wally continues. 'It's a way off still. But we've started production, whatever that means.'

Arne nods vacantly, his eyes distant and daughterwards.

Wally grins, gazing affectionately at his greying friend. He reads him, as always. 'She'll be alright.'

'You don't know that.'

'Have hope, Arne.'

They fall silent and let the ocean, gushing and heaving in all kinds of unseen horrors, do the talking.

'Why, Wal?'

'Why what?'

'Why should I have hope, knowing what we know?'

'Because it's the only way, right?'

'But that hope isn't real.'

'Hope is never real, Arne,' Wally states flatly, crossing his arms, raising one leg up behind him against the strut of the pier, burying his standing leg deeper into the sand. 'That's the point.'

Arne has nothing to say. He cannot see into his children's future. The rest of this century, and the next, disintegrate in his mind, beyond imagining. Near begging, he asks Wally, 'So what is it that gives you hope?'

'*Them*, Arne. They're different. Different to us. Different even to the ones just before them. They get it in a way we never could. Children of Greta. Climate kids. Call them what you will, but there's a kind of planetary consciousness coming through. So many of the old ways are collapsing—have been since the early twenties, sure—but, again, this feels different. They've opted out. They've seen through our bullshit, just like we did with boomers, except instead of just posting memes, they're doing something. A kind of digital disobedience, you might call it.'

Arne begins to shift uneasily in the sand, which is turning bronze and pewter beneath the mismatching bulbs of the streetlights—some new, others old and not yet replaced—of the beach road. 'But we've already done so much. We've barely begun to see the effects of everything we did. It's too late.'

'Most likely,' Wally sighs. 'But they are resilient, Arne. I know that means little in the midst of so much breakdown. But they just live. They've never known any other world. They see it as it is, not as it was.'

Arne recognises the truth of this, and it's all the more difficult to bear. Whenever Raph or Jasmine log on and cast some retro and verdant skin—one from the dad era—onto the walls of their home, it would hit him hard, while only forming a mere point of curiosity to them: *Is the world no longer this way?* To see his children taking this history of loss in their stride brought him great pain, but also shame.

They begin to stroll back towards Freddie and Jasmine.

'You guys are okay, right?' Wally enquires. 'Getting by?'

It's a loaded question. Wally knows how things have tightened. Stability, that flyaway dream, a constant anxious mirage. Evie, like Arne, worked seasonally for casualised and exploitative sources of labour. The only possibility for each of them, really. Under new government restrictions, there was no family-friendly tenure in research. And most of Evie's work came from faceless conglomerates wanting to do over the Earth's big blue bed.

'I'll help you guys, Arne,' Wally says.

'Isn't that part of the problem?' Arne asks, moving his hand back and forth between them to signify their bond, remembering some fragment from Wally's decades of drafting. 'Us and them. Ingroups and outgroups? No greater outgroup than the planet, or something like that.'

Delighted, Wally places a hand on Arne's back. 'So you were paying attention back then!'

'Well, you paid me to.'

Wally shrugs. 'To be honest, I've been rethinking that one—I'm not so sure anymore.'

'Well, I still have no idea what *The Chronicle* is, or what it does.'

'It's many things,' Wally says in an unnecessarily mysterious manner, clearly having fun. 'How many times do I need to explain it to you!'

'Yeah, yeah, yeah. Congrats anyway.'

'Don't congratulate me. I'm a small piece in it all. We're thinking of opening a headquarters here, actually. You could do research. Work on trees. Birds. Whatever you like.'

'Thanks, Wal,' Arne replies, concealing his preference for the real.

They arrive back to find Freddie and Jasmine cackling and discussing the stars above, now out in full swing, as clear as they ever were. The pair seem inverted, somehow. Freddie, small and cross-legged, fixated on his niece's every word; Jasmine, up on her knees, reaching for the stars, decoding ancient meanings out of light. Something has softened in Freddie during his years away. Maybe he's storing this moment, preserving it for harder times ahead.

Something plummets inside Arne, descending fast. Perhaps, after this, he will not see Freddie again, whose militancy is running deeper and deeper with each farewell. And there is a sense of finality about Freddie as he rises tall to his feet, placing a gentle hand on Jasmine's shoulder as they look out into the universe, prepared now for any end.

LATER THAT NIGHT, around the pixel-perfect glow of fire, a hearth with real heat conjured by Raph, they make merry. They all enjoy the ersatz expressions of Raph's work. Jasmine dabbles, also. Her work is subtle and more like her mother's—animal details, speckles of light and life. Arne wouldn't know where to begin.

Wally plays around with their interfaces, noting similarities to minor features of *The Chronicle* as he turns the Bakke household into an Amazonian canopy. Raph and Jasmine take turns, before working in delighted tandem. A woodland from long ago. Some vital estuary that was destroyed last year somewhere. Gumlands, impossibly endless, populated with koalas and detailed with platypus-rich rivers. They go back to the Tarkine, which makes Freddie, between sips of old brandy, morose. They move through a drowning city no one visits anymore. They travel back eons through ice cores to an impossibly old and cold Antarctica. They wind backwards and forwards through geology. Floods, fire and all manner of weather events, in between brief, idyllic scenes of planetary peace. They go on until the adults among them no longer can. Although addictive, it's exhausting work for those burdened by age.

Departing late, with Jasmine and Raph clawing at them, Freddie and Wally make plans to return throughout their stay in Melbourne. Arne offers them each a bed in their cramped unit, which they decline. Wally is staying at a fancy hotel along the raised Southbank, holding meetings with various 'stakeholders' in *The Chronicle*. And Freddie—Arne knows better than to try to talk to him about his plans in anything other than code.

They drop in several times that week. Ordering pizza—a rare treat. Beaming Evie into the house. Playing games. Reading. Watching old *Star Wars* movies from the aughts, the origins of these iconic characters thrilling Raph and Jasmine. It's a week of fun they each will, in time, remember as one of joy—the kind reserved solely for the sweet past.

But objects are left too. Mementos.

Freddie's leaving is silent and sobbing and without promises. When Raph and Jasmine return to their room they find identical badges of resistance, metallic and inexplicably heavy for their size, slipped beneath their pillows. By their uncle's farewell whisperings, they keep them secret—keep them safe—from their parents.

Wally sticks around for a couple of days and, although he plans to return soon enough, he makes a point of saying a proper farewell.

To Raph, he gifts a download code to *The Chronicle* in testing, along with a lifetime's suite of features for when it goes live. It's not clear whether Raph, with his mop of dark hair drifting across his face, is pleased or not; but at the very least Wally will be able to link in with him and see how he's going.

To Jasmine, he gifts something from a previous life: an acoustic guitar, once his favourite, glistening but for pick scratches across the soundboard. 'You have your mother's voice,' Wally explains, 'and with this you'll be undeniable.' It shines before her, the realest thing she's ever seen. She holds it up and decides then that she wants to sing songs for all her life. There's something else. A key taped to the headstock, which, Wally explains, will access a storage unit filled with his old gear, where she can make all the noise in the world and sing it anew.

9

STRIKE

Carbon dioxide parts per million: 581.2

Across the world, they flock to the streets of cities once more. Different school colours, different classes, they uniformly strike together on the same day. The Melbourne flock marches in heaving variegations—blazers of garish purple, red pinstripes on navy, dull greys, the odd unironed white shirt here and there—but all towards one place. The first wave of blazered high school students arrives near Parliament House at 11:58 am. They spring up the old sandstone steps and wind their way through the grand colonnades, engulfing the western entry in their chorus. In no awe of history, they declare the future theirs.

Over the next hour they come in their tens of thousands. Swelling droves, flowing out through the many city blocks. The buildings they move between bear the scars of the years' surges— hasty, patchwork repairs and, in the lower-lying parts of the city, floodmarks the height of small children—and yet they remain a generation bonded together in fear.

At 12:17 pm Jasmine emerges from Town Hall Station to a streetscape thronging with her kind. Endless schools of thought shifting in the currents, hurrying back and forth but within the tide—a generational gravity, pulling them, calling them to strike for their lives. It calls to Jasmine, too. She takes a moment, breathes it in, before looking up.

The day is unusually clear, almost clement, the sky radiating the forgotten blue of long-ago. Before the Long Heat and the restrictions. Before the energy coup. Before the season of asthma that, although she survived, stole her childhood, her cheery wonder. Before the storm surges, etched now into this city.

She falls in with the school strike, the human rapids flowing up Bourke Street towards Parliament House. She keeps a watchful eye out for Harper and Ava. At Exhibition Street the crowd grows unnavigable. She cannot get through to the front of the strike. She rapidly swipes the air.

> Jazzy: Where youse?
>
> Harps: We walkin up frm state library station. U?
>
> Jazzy: Got off @ town hall. Almost at parliament.
>
> Ava: Shoot us ya loc and we'll come find ya.
>
> Jazzy: Done! Hectic here. Packed. SO MANY PPL!
>
> Harps: Cool! there soon.

Jasmine waits.

Exposed by her stillness, the crowd rippling past her, she begins to tap her feet on the pavement. She prefers to be on the move nowadays. She focuses on the many emerging hives within the strike. Swarms of followers locate and encircle the influential among them, those with their heads in the cloud.

She didn't follow anyone here. She and Ava convinced Harper—@HarPerfect—to turn up unfollowed so they could do their own thing. Just the three of them, like in primary school. The Gang. Harper relented, later declaring to her followers that she would be offlining for the school strike, branding it 'grassroots' and 'old-school'. She cited hyperintegration as 'complicit and part of the problem' and implored her followers to do likewise. This grew her outreach and metrics significantly.

Spinning, Jasmine surveys the slogans floating and bobbing over the sea of heads. They project from the latest glass. Some, however, are rendered like hers: on dull cardboard. A 'placard', her father had called it as he, with cringeworthy enthusiasm, fashioned one for her earlier that morning. He also offered one of his old, primitive iPads, which, although she used it for basic games, would have been deeply embarrassing to brandish at the school strike. Cardboard and a permanent marker could at least pass for retro.

Jasmine scans the crowd, imbibing the colourful words that disappear and reappear in rapid kaleidoscopic visions:

Change the System, Not the Climate!

Tell Me About the GREAT Barrier Reef

Make Earth Great Again!

She unfolds the floppy scrap of cardboard from her backpack and, after considering it—*Save the Planet, Our Only Home*—for a moment, shoves it down a recycling bin, its lettering and therefore its meaning collapsing therein.

A weightlessness arrives. Jasmine feels she could breeze over to the front of the march right now but remains fixed, waiting for her friends. It's hard to stay still when the world is rushing, spiralling.

A voice comes starkly behind her. 'This is hope, babe!'

She turns around and is crushed by one of Ava's bearhugs, the ones she saves for reunions, lifting you up into the air and twirling you around, leaving you dizzy with love. When Ava sets Jasmine back down, the three girls form a triangular hug, into which they mumble various miss yous—the best of friends, the worst of times.

They update each other on many nothings, most of which they already know from each other's feeds. But some things need to be spoken, heard.

Harper starts to tear up.

'Oh, Harpsichord,' Ava teases, 'don't worry, you can have a big hug too.'

'Shut up!' Harper says, pushing Ava and wiping away her tears. 'Just miss the three of us hanging, that's all.'

'I know. How could you not miss me?' Ava sings, spinning

around in her chequered dress and dark blazer. 'But that's your fault for going to a fancy school, Harps!'

Growing up, Harper was one of the only kids Jasmine knew whose parents had permanent jobs. Her father also had one of those old petrol cars, which Jasmine, despite her own father's objections, always loved riding in. It smelled animally and minty. Harper's father had a heritage licence and could drive a certain quota of kilometres per month, which he routinely boasted about breaking—except for those months he was overseas—and paid the carbon fine. Rumour had it that he was unvaccinated, too. Inevitably, Harper's family moved to a wealthier, reportedly safer part of Melbourne. Higher ground, extra police and security.

Ava, whose high school is close to Harper's, still lives down the road from Jasmine but is kept busy by both the long commute home—the burden of brightness—and hours and mountains of homework, whose relevance and meaning, not long from now, will be wiped from Ava's consciousness on Melbourne's first fifty-degree day.

'We can't all be smart like you, Ava,' Harper says, before deferring to Jasmine. 'Right, Jazz?'

Jasmine shrugs. 'The fuck would I know?'

Harper and Ava exchange amused looks and quickly collapse into laughter. While they are distracted, Jasmine hurries a hand through her hair, retousling her tight curls, willing them to slope downwards across her brow, just so.

Ava turns quite suddenly on her heels back to Jasmine. 'State school's got you all rough,' she remarks. 'I like it.'

'Your school's a state school too,' Jasmine replies.

'Yeah, sort of. Not really. Know what I mean?'

Jasmine gives a tight little nod, remembering the day they both sat the Year Nine entrance exam. It was the same day her mother had departed once again, just as her father had earlier that year. The exhausting parental seesaw. This time it was to record what was considered by experts the final bleaching of the Great Barrier Reef.

And they were right. Those last sanctuaries were utterly reduced to everlasting bone, their coral flesh burned to ashen clumps of sea debris. Jasmine remembers the softness with which her mother placed a kiss on her forehead that morning on her way out, telling her that she was the brightest of stars, the most precious little being. Jasmine wrote not a single word that day.

Three days later their home flooded. Not as badly as the city and bayside areas, but enough to unnerve her generally sanguine father in a way only the weather could.

Harper leads Jasmine and Ava through the crowd, pausing every so often to crane her long neck in search of a way forward.

'Hey, giraffe!' Ava barks. 'What can you see?'

'I dunno. Looks like things are happening. Top of the steps. Whatsherface has a microphone.'

The crowd noise rises to a crescendo, the volume and pitch producing a sweeping harmonic that rings out as far as the inner suburbs. There's a visceral intensity in the air, a heightened sense. Alone, it feels like fear. But together, at this grand a scale, it feels like hope. Ava was right: hope does look like this.

For weeks the trio have been sharing old School Strike for Climate and Extinction Rebellion videos, flicking and scrolling right back to 2018, a couple of years before things went haywire. Change and lack of change at once. More than twenty years, accelerated and flickering in the dark of their bedrooms, distilled through objects made only for looking. Hope and hopelessness bound together, the latter stalking the former. You could see it everywhere. *Only a hopeless world needs hope*—Jasmine slid that gem into her thoughts folder. The three of them cascaded down threads and subthreads old and new, catching fragments:

these kids are amazing we don't deserve them
sixth extinction event
Coronavirus—the Wuhan Flu!
carbon parts per million.
these brainwashed kids should be in school

The Great Reset
these kids will save us, resource scarcity
Black lives matter
All lives matter!
climate change is a hoax. Deep State. 5G
QAnon
vaccine mandates are against the Geneva Convention
The Great Awakening
Rising temperatures
life-denying system and ecocide
Pfizer. Adrenochrome!
the great acceleration
why didn't we save rhinos when we still could?
The end times

They went deeper, link by link, spiralling down the rabbit hole of algorithms. At least they were together through this. Jasmine felt able to take the lead and, with distant curiosity, navigate them through the murk. Denialists on 16chan calling for militant action against a new wave of climate policies. Ecologically minded porn on anthropornscene.com. Viral bedroom fascists. Men priming another generation of men to be angry at whatever—pandemic restrictions, a new vaccine, the ways in which total strangers online lived and identified, the latest iteration of wireless internet, climate refugees.

It was startling how quickly you could travel here. Just a few swipes. And this was just the surface. It went on and on, plummeting to even weirder depths. At times they lost Harper, who seemed to veer elsewhere before returning and maintaining course. Although she never said it, Jasmine sensed Raph's presence here too, the faint outlines of his edgy, contrarian lexicon.

She pushes all this down and tries to catch some of Ava's infectious, giddying hope. Hand in hand, they push to the front, which, when they reach it, is jostling with a ferocity not present farther back. A speaker, not even a few years older than them, takes to the stage and instils widespread calm. She is magnetic, her voice like the middle of a pillow. Ava whispers undying love: 'I want to marry that woman.' Jasmine and Harper stifle their giggles, suffering several looks of admonishment from the sweet and sincere among them.

Quiet arrives. The wind lingers around the speaker. It sings strangely in her midst. Her stole, entwined chicly around her neck and down her left arm, flickers with practised importance, as if she has waited for just this very moment to shepherd the flock—hundreds of thousands of them, it will later be reported. She takes a final measured and choreographed step towards the microphone and declares, 'Let's remember this.'

An old tune rings out—Jasmine recognises it as one of Uncle Wally's favourite bands. A sprinkling of piano notes and stirring strings and, lilting through it, that sobering voice from long ago, speaking of future horrors that have now long since passed:

> *We are right now in the beginning of a climate and ecological crisis.*
>
> *And we need to call it what it is. An emergency.*
>
> *We must acknowledge that we do not have the situation under control and that we don't have all the solutions yet. Unless those solutions mean that we simply stop doing certain things.*
>
> *We must admit that we are losing this battle.*
>
> *We have to acknowledge that the older generations have failed. All political movements in their present form have failed.*
>
> *But* Homo sapiens *have not yet failed.*
>
> *Yes, we are failing, but there is still time to turn everything around. We can still fix this. We still have everything in our own hands.*
>
> ...
>
> *We can create transformational action that will safeguard the living conditions for future generations.*

Or we can continue with our business as usual and fail.
That is up to you and me.

And yes, we need a system change rather than individual
change. But you cannot have one without the other.

If you look through history, all the big changes in society
have been started by people at the grassroots level. People
like you and me.

...

Everything needs to change. And it has to start today.
So, everyone out there, it is now time for civil disobedience.
It is time to rebel.

The words echo and carom off buildings above the thunder of the
crowd. They yearn for change and justice. It only makes sense.
They have come up helpless beneath a legacy of infinite wrongs.
Increased growth, ceaseless living, boundless being, running its
course on a finite planet—a star, once an island of refuge in the
empty sea of space.

Harper slams her hands over her ears, wincing. Ava rolls her
eyes and teases her. It's not that bad; she could do with a bit more
noise in her life. Jasmine cuts in between them and links arms.
Their blazers—particularly Harper's—are enviously soft against
her skin. She could sleep squished there between them. Wake to
a better world after all this has settled. But she has rebelling to
do, and the world cannot wait.

Somehow Jasmine manages to remain linked with Harper and
Ava in the roiling crowd, dragging them through a field of jutting
hips and elbows, and up the parliamentary steps, coming to a halt
just metres from the stage. She asks Harper to lift her up.

'What?' Harpers yells in confusion.

Ava chimes in. 'Lift her up, ya big dumb sexy bitch!'

Harper looks at them and shrugs, *Okay*. She gets down to her
knees and raises Jasmine onto her shoulders, lifting her up above
the height of the protest. The scale of the surging crowd makes

Jasmine dizzy. A multitude with no edge, proceeding forever. She steadies herself, breathes through the vertiginous feeling, then commands Harper to move up one or two steps. Harper lurches forward, forcing Jazz into an unstable tilt until she manages to plant her feet on the plinth of one of the elaborate lampposts that line Parliament House.

'What the are you doing?' Harper shrieks, struggling in a near-horizontal bend from the waist up, but laughing deep within her ribcage as Jasmine reaches out and wraps her arms around the thick stem of the lamppost, alighting there. Ava is losing her shit, capturing all of this.

Jasmine begins to ascend.

'You're a mad woman!' yells Ava, cupping her hands around her mouth. 'But that's why I love you!' She then turns to Harper, who is trying to collect herself. 'Look at her go. Do you think she knows we can see up her skirt?'

'Don't think she cares,' Harper says, still catching her breath. 'She's possessed.'

Jasmine now dangles from the top of the lamppost, wedged monkey-like into one of the ornate structure's two thin, curved arms that extend sideways, each housing a large, clear lightbulb at their end, distinct from the whitened bulb at the top and centre of the post. From this vantage, the strike takes on a different form: it is a single, powerful entity made up of school students, but also, in greater number than in years before, the entire city. There are all manner of people here, thudding and unwavering, more regiment than rally. So much could go right and wrong from this moment—a great transformation or the beginning of the end. Or something in between, an earthly limbo.

Jasmine senses something on the wind, a strange whirr in the distance. She suddenly feels all too visible. The wind wants to sway her, shake her to the ground. She retreats, swinging around the lamppost and sliding down to the plinth, where Harper helps her climb down.

A News Corp chopper comes around, swinging low. Too low. It then conducts a wider sweep of the city to capture the troublesome crowd to beam back to other places where protest is no longer permitted. When it returns for a second pass, it pauses over the stage, focusing on the leaders. Harper pulls her glass from her bag and swipes through several slogan templates before finally settling on one, which she personalises with her own particular purple and leafy green touch, projecting it high in the air: *We Are the Future.*

Something plummets inside Jasmine. She and Ava share a silent, knowing look. Something gnawing, unsettling. The irreversible flow of history. They won't go to bed weeping tonight—as with the previous generation's epidemic of eco-anxiety, which eased as hope became more and more impossible—but they will morbidly log in to play *Civilization* and, in just a couple of hundred turns, solve the climate crisis. It's painfully easy. Jasmine and Ava make a great team and almost always elect to pursue victory through science, striving for utopia more out of want than guile. It's much harder to win by domination—the game design discourages it—but it is, at a primal level, still fun, and ends in rapturous flood and fire. In years to come they will increasingly choose this option, deliberately losing and cheering with ecstatic, apocalyptic relief as civilisation collapses, exorcising the greatest burden of their lives for a flickering moment.

And as for Harper—well, she cannot afford to appear in despair, trading as she does in a brand of embodied hope, a positive greenness that her father, although disapproving, is relieved she has managed to make profitable. Even if she does donate some of that profit to climate initiatives, at least she is stimulating markets, however puerile they might be.

At 3:14 pm the gathering begins to dissipate. That initial inflow of hope and excitement now flows out, bounced around in networks, exchanges, conversations on homeward journeys. Just a frisson, the moment of community that took place here.

For tomorrow will be the same as yesterday, and true change will remain a chimera, the fantastical plaything of stories.

Although she does not know it yet, Jasmine will, in decades to come, feel with a burning sensation that days like today mattered. That the all-too-slow rebellion that arose over time did ultimately save something, its legacy budding in those slowly rewilding pockets of the planet. But for now it's 3:51 pm on a school day and the world still might become anything.

Not wanting to say goodbye, they linger in the emptying streets. They locate and catch up with friends and cousins and crushes, mucking around and watching the protest turn to nothing, its aftermath a slowly passing mystery. A group of younger girls strolls past, asking for a photo with Harper. She obliges. They ask what the strike was like and Jasmine, Harper and Ava each relate that it was amazing, transcendent. The younger girls' elite school banned its students from attending, under threat of expulsion. The girls then ask no one in particular: 'What happens next?'

No one seems to know, until Harper finally explains: 'We do it again.'

Eventually the best friends part ways, heading in different directions. Harper proceeds to the edge of the gardens that skirt Parliament House and waits for her father to pick her up. Ava trams it to one of the city libraries to study, yelling on her way, 'Later tonight, let's win. I'm in a winning mood, Jazzy!'

Jasmine nods, smiling.

Once alone, Jasmine weaves through what little of the crowd remains and slips away towards the Carlton Gardens, skipping by the Exhibition Building and museum. She brings up some beats and tunes out, bouncing along the footpaths and gliding between the trees. Upright conifers. Elms lined like sentries. Fairytale figs. Enduring oaks, far from their homeland. Eucalypts, endlessly old and cradling the story of the Earth: great floods and ice ages and, in their roots, fire. Jasmine brushes by, pressing her palms against them until their bark flesh pinches hers.

A galah, pink and grey and searching, pecks around the base of the biggest of the oaks. It unravels a feeling within. A memory, faint and difficult to tweeze. She reaches in and plucks it out, a sharp sensation that Raph had once chased her around this very oak when they were little. The tree—*Quercus robur*—remains unchanged.

It was autumn, and the drifts carried the smell of wet earth, urging trees to shake down their crimsoning litterfall. A family picnic, maybe. Yes. Mum and Dad were sitting on opposing corners of a rug, distant. Raph was hurtling after her. Really, she was leading him, exaggerating her sisterly terror.

They spun around the immense white oak in tightening circles, giggling frantically as they clamoured together over its foot of roots, raising their palms to the tree to right themselves before this noble giant. Little Jasmine quietened, as did Raph. She stepped back and, catching her breath, considered the colossal being before her. She turned to sit with her back against the tree's gnarled surface, its living sapwood gushing with unspeakable force inches beneath, transporting hundreds of litres of water and nutrients upward. Growing unnoticed. Moving at the speed of wood, of deeper, vaster ages greater than human civilisation's recent progress. The tree took Jasmine's weight. She patted the damp, leafy spot beside her, inviting Raph to sit.

But there's something else in the memory. She remembers asking Raph why the tree had a large plastic cuff wrapped around its trunk—as it still does—and he said it was to stop the tree from escaping. She asked Raph if he knew what the tree did wrong, and he said that he did but couldn't tell her because the story was too horrible.

'That doesn't sound right,' Jasmine snorted.

'It is. Just listen to me, okay. I'm older.'

'Maybe it's to stop kids from climbing it.'

'That's stupid. They'd still be able to climb it. Bet you I could.'

He couldn't.

The galah rears its head up now, curious about Jasmine's presence. Its plumage ripples crisply as it takes wing, disappearing in the hazy, pinkening glow of the evening. The city pulses with the electric flow of traffic. Suits flurry about importantly.

At 4:45 pm Jasmine is notified of a message from her father. It flashes through the air before her—Wow! Incredible crowd. You kids are so switched on. All of you, amazing. Where are you? Proud of you, Jazzy ♥. But she wants to be left alone. She turns everything off, tuning down to her surroundings.

A force beyond hearing hums in the heart of the oak, which she leans into. Quite suddenly, she realises she is digging a heel into a notch in the trunk, climbing the tree her older brother once could not.

After a few negotiations—repivots and three-points-of-contact speculations—Jasmine is ensconced in the crown of the oak. The tree embraces her, its branches tighten with breathing. Kneeling there out of view, she hears all kinds of people passing through below, talking of the strike. Not just school students, but parents and teachers and the elderly and the homeless. They express a fear she recognises as her own. If only they'd felt it decades ago.

Jasmine shifts in her queendom of branches. She responds to her father at 5:25 pm—I'm in a tree! Got gr8 view of things. If ya see me on the news climbing a lamppost I'm not sorry. actually heaps of you old ones were there today right?! dont try loc me I'll see you at home 4 dinner later xox.

Jasmine makes a speedy descent from the oak and heads for Parkville Station. On the train home, chugging west out of Arden, it begins to rain, which makes Jasmine want to reach out to her mum. Just for a minute. But she's offnet, hard to find. It's meant to be her last trip—but that's a worn-out promise. Jasmine rests her head against the cool of the window and, from blurrily close, traces her forefinger along the droplets sweeping along the outside of the glass, imagining a different world, dreaming of ways to escape.

HE SPOTS THEM. Perched on a bench, the Prinsengracht trembling at their feet, they whisper terrible things of now and tomorrow. Four hands cupped together, peering into a screen—Kim's, John guesses, since she arranged the catch-up. He imagines that Freddie is an increasingly deviceless man nowadays, with Kim running errands that would make a younger version of herself retch. But he is speaking for her when he ought not. He need not lower himself to hearsay and aspersion when the facts sit before him, across the canal. Still, he rates the odds of gossip in the subchat tonight with Wally—and even Arne or Evie if he can reel them in with the right banter—to be good.

Halfway over the bridge, John pauses. He breathes in the dying light, the candled play of Amsterdam's colours, brilliant against the black of the canal's new tide, held back—for now—by years of adaptation, floodwalls the likes of which most of the world has suffered without. Tomorrow he will deliver his keynote at the climate summit, and all he can think is how the various and nefarious happenings and deal-makings this week could have been plucked from any previous summit, going back decades.

He closes his eyes, glides his hands back and forth along the metal railing, the first dew of the evening setting in. He goes even deeper and wishes he were home, long as it has been. Hopping from university to university, he has lost track of the moments—which is ironic, given the painstaking documenting that goes into his work. How long has it been? He has seen Kim a few times over the years, but it must have been a decade or more since he last laid eyes on Freddie's dumb, angular face. Pulling up the collar of his topcoat and thrusting his hands deep into his front pockets, he strolls towards them as nonchalantly as he can manage.

They spot him, earlier than he would have liked. They leap up and roar in delight, waiting for him to enter their familiar embrace. John asks what they were watching so keenly on Kim's device. She pulls him in to watch the highlights: the latest school climate protests, including in Melbourne, where they catch a glimpse of Jasmine, in stark contrast to her brother, pulling off some striking antics. A proud yet distant uncle and aunt, the pair of them.

I'm more her uncle than youse'll ever be, John thinks, before collecting himself, softening before Kim, who gestures to the bench.

For a flash, John plays through how much time the two of them had spent together as postgrads. How close they were. Their long fieldtrips to strange parts of the world, generally under the wing of Professor Hadley, with whom John has remained in touch, the old rebel fading out of academia and, more recently, into a life of action. It isn't something John dwells on much, but as he takes in the glorious greys streaking through Kim's dark shock of hair, he knows there was something there once. Maybe that's the only reason Freddie is here.

Kim pulls a box of miniature Dutch-style apple pies out from her satchel, offering them up with black coffee from a thermos, which she distributes into three tin mugs. John has been gulping these pastries all week, their streusel topping a work of art.

They sit side by side—Kim in the middle—exchanging vital trivialities for what seems like forever. Long enough to usher in the dark, at least. Kim offers John another pour, which he accepts gladly, despite having never particularly liked the stuff. But, for whatever reason, coffee always seems to make people talk. He has used it countless times over the years as a researcher to ease into a conversation.

'So what brings you here?' John asks. 'You didn't come all the way to Amsterdam just for me.'

Kim and Freddie share a furtive look, a back-and-forth registered in the minute facial expressions of coupledom.

'Well,' Kim begins, 'who's to say we wouldn't come all this way just to see you, John?'

Charmed only for a second, John scoffs. They share an awkward laugh, their truths unfolding in silences.

Kim's features harden abruptly, her eyes setting to still and lethal. 'You know,' she says, and John averts his gaze downstream and into the darkness. 'You know, don't you?'

In John's periphery Freddie's silhouette appears to enlarge, rise. John imagines the life Kim might have had were it not for Freddie. Then again, when he looks up now, taking them both in, he feels the temptation, and even the efficacy, of fear. In many ways they were right; yet, even after decades of pondering the question, John has never been able to reconcile violence, even for the planet's sake—even for life's sake.

In recent years there has been a string of coordinated, targeted strikes, going to the top of the fossil fuel companies and big tech. Often with collateral damage. Left unclaimed, rumour—crafted and manufactured, John deduced—circulated throughout the web of things, giving the movement infinite forms, limitless potential. That potential is now forming in the shadows, its pieces clear to see if you were looking at the world close enough, as John has been.

Kim places a hand on John's knee. 'We want you to come with us. We could do with people like you.'

'People like me?' John says, unsure as to whether he should be flattered or offended. 'The fuck do you mean by that?'

'Thinkers!' Freddie groans from behind Kim, looking off into the distance, emptying his mind. 'There are a great number of us now, ready to act. Good people—many barely adults—flocking to fight for the world. But we need people who can think, who can lead.'

'You're fucking joking, right? You need a philosopher in your terrorist ranks? Fuck me.' John lurches forward and rests his elbows on his knees, digging his fingers into his pounding head.

'That's not what this is,' Kim says, her voice softer now. John is sure he detects sadness. 'Trust me. Please.'

He wants to—there is nothing he would rather do. He wants to ask why he should trust her, but he cannot.

Time turns strange in the rolling cold, visibility dwindling. Maybe it's seconds, maybe minutes, but John speaks clearly. 'I wish I could. But I can't.'

'We fight for the same thing, brother!' Freddie insists, leaning over Kim.

'Don't you fucking call me that, you cunt.' John leaps up and starts pacing back and forth. A strange desire to jump into the Prinsengracht comes over him. 'You and I, Freddie—we've never fought for the same thing. Don't kid yourself that you're saving the world. You're just bringing more violence into it.'

'John, ple—'

'Let him vent,' Freddie interjects, extending an arm across Kim.

'Shut up, you condescending prick,' John fires. 'You always were a bastard.' He turns to Kim, now begging. 'Kim, you don't have to go this way.'

And there, in resounding finality, words fail. John stands awkwardly before them, looking down, toes dancing back and forth over the pavement. He suspects it's all gone as Freddie hoped. Planned.

Kim rises to her feet and moves to within inches of John. He can smell her breath. Over her shoulder, Freddie reclines, somehow relaxed as ever, here at 581.2 parts per million, the last time John checked. Kim starts to play with the collar of his coat, smoothing it, straightening things up.

'I know you think that I follow him,' she intones, tilting her head back towards Freddie, who is now horizontal and puffing fist-sized clouds of carbon dioxide up into the air. 'But I do not.'

'Okay,' John manages, taken aback.

'Don't presume.'

'I won't…I'm sorry.'

'No, you're not, John,' she decides, looking at him fondly. 'And that's okay.'

'What?' he says, lost.

'We see things differently. I thought—hoped—we might not, but here we are. At the end.'

'The end?'

'Yes, John. This is goodbye.'

John reaches out to her, cradling a shoulder. 'Do you know what you're doing?'

She takes a moment, one in which John is sure he senses conflict. But he retreats.

'I do.'

With that, Freddie rises stiffly, readying to take their leave. He edges up beside Kim and takes her hand. Without so much as a warning they march off into the night, Kim mouthing *Goodbye* on her way, to which John manages only to raise a hand, empty but for a chestful of things he wants to say but never will.

10

16CHAN

Carbon dioxide parts per million: 583.24

Deep_state_9: K guys. Lez discuss this one. I've seeded a cloud. Check it. If the seed doesn't work—I know this keeps happening—here's a link to the article for those brave enough to try an old browser.

Atmosfears11: haha the internet.

BigDikSmlGov88: Oh gawd. You really wanna integ with this crap? The guy literally knows nothing about the earth sciences. Was a shitty muso and he's a hack who hasn't written anything good in years. The homo got to where he is by sleeping around high places. It's true. Look it up. not that there's anything wrong with that. power to the guy. fuck who you like, so long as it's not me! But yeah…ppl considering plugging into this need to get their meds upped.

CatastRaphe: Ooh boi do I have something for you guyz.

Atmosfears11: wot.

CatastRaphe: I have access to this.

Deep_state_9: bull. why would you lie like that for everyone here to see

CatastRaphe: No seriously. I've had it for years while it was in dev. It's a whole network of its own, endless interactive climate content. A compendium. I'll flick caps to a dark cloud. You know the one. Dive in.

> **Deep_state_9:** Sure you will. What's next, climate change is real?

> **BigDikSmlGov88:** Guys leave CatastRaphe alone. He's super cereal

> **Atmosfears11:** haha old jk but still good value

Indiana_DowJones: You? Some rando—no offence—has access to a multi-million-dollar immersion UX that has been shrouded in secrecy for what, decades?

Atmosfears11: He's gone. Don't think he'll be coming bak anytime soon.

Indiana_DowJones: Who the fuck would buy this anyway? Biggest money-making scam in history. Give us your money and we will stop it! Lol

Stan4Reason: Have you read the article? It's going to be free. Open access. I'm for this really. As long as it's done right and CC isn't just shoehorned in there and rammed down our throats.

Indiana_DowJones: Yeah whatever, bet they'll throw up a paypoint after release. Throw all the money at it you like, Stan4.

Stan4Reason: What are you even talking about! Do you hear yourself? You're basing that on nothing but spec.

Indiana_DowJones: Wevs. Go ahead and drink the green jew-juice, bruh. Won't matter in the end. Just helping the Rich rise into their towers while the rest of us down here are taxed to death, drowning.

> **BigDikSmlGov88:** Preach!

Stan4Reason: So you admit CC is happening!

Indiana_DowJones: The climate has always been changing and humans have very little impact on that. Everyone should treat the Earth well and take care of it, but the idea that cow farts melted the ice caps is beyond nonsense. No one is doubting that there's pollution or smog that's bad for us and the weather is getting more and more fukt. But the idea that humans (or cows) have changed the temperature of the planet is super vein of us. We aren't that important.

> **Atmosfears11:** I think you have a bovine fetish buddy

> **Indiana_DowJones:** Seen! I wish I didn't. Can barely afford that shit these days.

Deep_state_9: Yea we all heard this bullshit the first time when they called it "Global Warming" like 50 years ago. Then they came up with like 20 other alarm whistles for CC. I can't even keep up with these fakes anymore. Are we in a collapse? escalation? breakdown? catastrophe? acceleration? They're not even clear on the narrative. Anyone who hands more money over to the gov and the elite for something mythical needs to go blow their brains out.

ChemTails: I'm not even willing to agree we could affect the climate. Scientists can't even show how we can affect the weather. We've also had higher CO_2 in the past and they can't tell us what temp the Earth should be to start with. It's all just power grab scam for power and money.

BigDikSmlGov88: Yeah, like how much money would colleges lose if "man-made" CC is proven false? All those "scientists" would be out of jobs and the grants would dry up. There are piles of money to be made when you have a crisis or pandemic, ask the big pharmas. Why wouldn't 99% of climate scientists agree that global warming is real and man-made? Science is made to be questioned, but not climate science, disagree and you are out.

Stan4Reason: Umm have you guys looked outside lately? CC is quite clearly happening. But today's eco-fascists are blaming man entirely. Sure we might be a part of it, but not to the degree the children of Greta would have us believe. I'd like to know more, of course. And I'm open to being convinced otherwise. But from what I understand CO_2 is not a pollutant and there is just as much evidence saying that higher CO_2 levels are actually good for the environment. Carbon dioxide is tree food, right. Climate change is a trillion-dollar industry so of course propaganda is going to be coming from all directions saying it's happening and we/fossil fuels are the cause. Believe what you want obviously but don't be naive. Go look at the record—yes CC is happening, but I'm not sold on the attribution entirely. Hey, soon we'll be able to go deep on that with this Chronicle thing and maybe draw our own conclusions.

    Atmosfears11: Oh I'm sure you'll go deep on it

    BigDikSmlGov88: Tight lol

    Atmosfears11: CC is a hoax, stop pushing this crap 4Stan!

Indiana_DowJones: Listen, I'm all for recycling and finding a more intuitive way of producing electricity. there's no point not to, right? But it has to be done economically responsibly. But yeah this climate mob is getting to the point of religious fanaticism—all began in the 10s and 20s with Greta, if you ask me. Like did you see those school kids marching in the streets—terrorists in the making right there. And now with these climate crime laws popping up, I'm scared of where things are heading.

Stan4Reason: This is only slightly better than the flat out denial takes above. At least you somewhat acknowledge the realty of the situation which I didn't think was a huge hurdle to climb. But I agree with you—things are getting extreme. Stay safe out there!

Indiana_DowJones: Well, I mean there's still plenty of opportunities with CC (regardless of what is causing it). To innovate and make things work better. But also opportunities to seize— Antarctica, higher grounds, floodzone tourism, the north passage opening, etc. The Reef had its most visitors in its final years. Adaptation is key. There's no going back. we move on. Hey, We're going to Mars! It's not all doom and gloom.

BigDikSmlGov88: You can just guarantee us norms won't see any of that pie. It's all for the green elite. The irony. We're told to not drive, not eat meat, not have kids, all while influentials fly around in those old jet planes, live in safe-zone mansions and so on.

Greg: I'm just sad about all this. I don't even know what's true anymore. I'm just worried CC is going to kill me.

> **Atmosfears11:** Shut up Greg! No one cares what you think. Go suck a leaf.

> **Deep_state_9:** Yeah Greg. Get the fuck out of here.

> **Stan4Reason:** Bit much guys.

FossilApostle: You're all drifting off topic. Back to what Deep State seeded, this Climate Chronicle UX sounds like garbage island. I don't even understand what it is.

> **Atmosfears11:** I don't think anyone does, to be honest. Sounds like a total mess.

> **Greg:** Is it a game or an inferface? Or a full integration? I'm genuinely curious.

> **Stan4Reason:** It's not a game per se, it seems. It seems to afford quite a lot of features from what I can gather. Sounds impossibly large, if I'm being honest.

> **Atmosfears11:** Or how about keep politics out of stories, especially games. I don't want to be preached to while I

am trying to relax and escape. The entire point of games is to separate yourself from the problems of the real world

Stan4Reason: Firstly, I disagree. And again, I don't think it's a game exactly. Has anyone apart from me and Deep State read the piece?

    Greg: Just going through it now.

    ChemTails: Shut up Greg!

    Atmosfears11: haha what have I done. It's catching on

BigDikSmlGov88: Nope. TL;DR.

Atmosfears11: CC will kill us all before I get through this lol

Deep_state_9: The guy is seriously deluded if he thinks people are going to use this. Prob why the hack made it free. The state of him! Imagine your life's work being so bad you have to give it away for free.

BigDikSmlGov88: I'm on the side of cleaning the planet up don't get me wrong it actually really saddens me to see the amount of pollution ruining the oceans and killing the wildlife but keep that shit away from gaming.

Stan4Reason: Again, not a game. It's something entirely different.

Atmosfears11: Who does this Weatherall guy think he is? Kojima?

    ChemTails: How dare you utter them in the same breath!

    Atmosfears11: I would never.

BigDikSmlGov88: Ok Reasonable Stanley, what exactly is The Climate Chronicle then? That title is pure vomit by the way.

Stan4Reason: Dunno. He describes some of its features, without going into great detail. Carbon real-time overlay filters. Temporal augments. Solution modules. Customisable data vis. There's a "game-like" walkthrough that when asked the length of, he gets vague. But mostly he describes it as a connective and communication tool for an age of catastrophe. He uses a beehive to describe this, but like, I don't even know what that means. Here's a Wik on bees and beehives I found, for those who don't know. I think I get what he's saying and I'm curious to check it out.

> **Greg:** Me too!

Atmosfears11: Wow I'm dying here haha. What a tool. The only catastrophe here is this dumb game or whatever the fuck it is. Just what I want in my escapism…a game educating me on the political pseudo-science of man-made CC. The nerve.

Deep_state_9: Climate changes Stan, that doesn't mean our planet is doomed. It means the climate changes, which is always how it's been. Stop letting THEM control you over obvious stuff.

Green_Jedi: Climate reacts to whatever forces it to change at the time; humans are now the dominant forcing.

Atmosfears11: Who the fuck let this guy in? Where'd he come from?

> **Green_Jedi:** She.

> **Greg:** Me. I invited her.

>> **BigDikSmlGov88:** Goddammit Greg! This is meant to be a sealed space. You've ruined everything.

>> **ChemTails:** Classic Greg.

>> **Green_Jedi:** Leave him be. It's all of you who are lost.

Atmosfears11: Deep_State, you can drop this Jedi guy yeah? And Greg too while you're at it?

Greg: Sorry, guys.

> **Green_Jedi:** It's not your fault, Greg. This is a sick place. You're better off elsewhere.

Deep_state_9: Working on it.

Stan4Reason: No wait, let's hear the Jedi out.

FossilApostle: Calling climate change a global catastrophe is a joke. People like you, Jedi, are truly insufferable.

> **BigDikSmlGov88:** Oh shit, this guy! FossilApostle!

Green_Jedi: I never called it a catastrophe, but if you can't see it for what it is, then you are lost.

FossilApostle: Right…And so what if the ice is melting and oceans rising. You have to remember, those icebergs weren't here when the Earth was created necessarily. They came over time. Time which included drastic changes which are still happening to this day.

The folly. To think we can actually change mother nature's path

Humans won't destroy the planet. That's just fucking stupid. Humans will destroy themselves. Earth will still be here. It's been through multiple climate changes, and mass extinctions. The only thing that will destroy this planet is a dying sun.

These are all part of His plan. Fossil fuels are a gift for our brief time here. Use them wisely, sure, but use them still.

> **Atmosfears11:** Damn. That was intense. Not sure I agree with everything but respect the energy.

Green_Jedi: Amazing. Every word of what you just said was wrong.

Deep_state_9: Executing Order 66.

> **Indiana_DowJones:** This is huge. What are you doing exactly?

Atmosfears11: He's ejecting him, you downer. Oh my god. I'm sweating.

Greg: No, wai—

Green_Jedi: You are traitors to the clim—

ChemTails: Oh wow…

BigDikSmlGov88: …

Stan4Reason: …

CatastRaphe: Hey guys, I'm back. Take a look in the darkcloud. You'll find a playthrough I've made. Sorry, took a while to upload. What did I miss?

11
WEATHERALLS

Carbon dioxide parts per million: 611.67

In a city as old as scripture, accustomed to centuries of unending warmth, people shift their lives indoors and underground. The continent, gemmed with myriad improbable histories, yields this year to ice. The ocean—bringer and breaker of life—has come to a stall, its immense, abiding currents trapped in Arctic meltwater as deep formations run amok. Where beings—scientists, tourists, cetaceans—held funerals for glaciers over the decades, they now do so for the swelling ocean, destined to take cities down with it to Atlantis.

Deep in the heart of the ancient city, ruled by many empires and now by none, passing the cathedral and then the university, Wally clops along the cobblestones, those obdurate markers of time. Night is falling and the ice creeps deeper into his core. Ageless, he's still not quite prepared for this and could die out here soon enough.

He seeks a rumoured happening.

He slips into an underground spot, winging in on code, credential and vibe, and makes his way to the glow of the bar and perches on a stool. He orders *güisqui*, removing his techwear coat. Anticipation, youthful and abundant, pours over him—a sparkle like that of first flings, new experiences. The world as it was. Something deeply human is about to go down, older than language, greater than words. The prospect of actual live music sends an electricity—nostalgia—through him, fuzzy and familiar, from a former, gigging life. He leans towards the young, lithe bartender—born in the early thirties, Wally guesses—and asks, '¿A que hora comienza la tocada?'

The bartender chuckles at this old man, cringing. He vocodes idiomatically. It cracks a little—'Lo sient'—before his translated voice cuts through '—rry, needs updating. Don't strain yourself, Gev. Use your vox.'

Pushing away from the bar, Wally says he'd rather the young man deal with his broken Spanish.

'Suit yourself,' comes the reply. 'I'll still use mine. Times are changing, güero.'

They trade names as Wally gets up, folding his coat over his arm. After a moment he turns back to the bartender in contemplation. He vocodes: 'How could you tell?'

The young man—Ignacio—flattens his palms along the top of the bar, his biceps bulging. 'A lucky guess.'

Wally smiles, shaking his head. 'Nah, that's not it. Indulge me.' He decides to hover, ordering another drink. 'What gave me away for a Gev?'

The young man looks around the bar at the patrons coming in from the ice-world outside, before relenting. 'You have the look.'

'The look...so, you get Lifers coming through here, then?'

'No, not really. Might be an old city, but it's mainly *us* nowadays. The scholars have stayed, though.'

'You're a student?'

He nods, sombre.

'What are you studying?'

'Emissionography.'

Wally gives an approving nod. He tries to appear generationally self-aware, but shame, right and true, curls up inside, rendering him expressionless. He catches himself. Resisting the urge to say something patronising—*Well, good for you, we need people like you!*—

he asks once again, this time unaided: '*¿A que hora comienza la tocada?*'

'*En una hora.*'

Wally can hardly wait an hour to see her, the bearer of that mellifluous voice singing her heart out. The runaway child, living her best life here on the other side of the world.

It didn't take him long to find her. She might have clouded off, but no one is truly cloudless anymore. Not even her uncle Freddie could pull that off. We are all traceable, he had concluded, the last time they spoke.

Wally tunes out for so long, staring wearily into the bottom of his glass, that he does not at first see the hundreds flood in, cramming towards the front of the venue and through a portal into the band room. He slips some Reminiscence into his drink and follows the inflow.

Sliding through the portal, he is blown away by the sheer size of the interior space. He looks back and realises it is a short tunnel, leading to the concrete basement of a building conceivably adjacent to the bar. An augmentation, surely. Some shimmering, photorealistic conjuration from a previous carefree age of warehouse raves. But no—these people and their pilgrimage are real, present. And quite suddenly he is here too, self-oriented despite the Remmys, struck with an energy that has been dormant since before these young people—children that they are—were born.

Out of nowhere, lights begin to strobe in time with the loping thunder of a timpani and then go out. Darkness, total and perfect. The faint blue outlines of several figures creep forward, gargoyle-like as they take to their eclectic array of instruments, ancient and modern in equal measure. Some Wally knows intimately, others he's never seen before.

Through the darkness he is hit by a wall of thrilling sound. Brilliant light rises and falls. Holos, conjurations and old-school wall projections bounce around the room. Everyone else knows what's happening but he is sensorially lost, out of step and disastrously out of time. Despite his recently acquired longevity, he feels disastrously old. Sonically, it's like nothing else; his mind has no referent for what is unfolding, blasting his face, caroming around the underground. It bears irreconcilable intervals and cadences. The BPM is wide-ranging and erratic, the instrumentation a dissonant melange.

No one else seems to notice. Almost entirely without a tonic centre, those juiced up and pulsating around him go hard to the array of tones and flavours. Rhythms rise and fall like the most extreme weather, but the crowd somehow forecasts it, keeping up throughout. Pulses crescendo and collapse, polyrhythmic and arrhythmic in unequal measure. Decorated digitally in the skins of recent extinctions, the band succumbs to chaos and flux. Their semblances—the latest batch of anthropomorphic accessory, downloadable and infinitely customisable—thrill in their verisimilitude, if you could remember the koala, rhino and leopard.

But where is she?

Each changeling child seems disconnected from the band whole, playing independently of one another, until, after far too many minutes of anarchy for even Wally's once-experimental likings, a voice, honeylike and serene, cuts through, interconnecting all the separate limbs—drums, guitars, a fretless bass, a Fender Rhodes, an electric violin, a rotating battalion of alien instruments, a vintage Kaoss Pad, various other effects units and interfaces, as well as a handful of new-fangled contraptions he had never seen before—across this flailing basement.

And there she is, an eagle coming through the light. One of her father's lost birds, rummaging for sounds, assembling them into some majestic sonic tapestry.

And then, inexplicably, she detonates it all, sends it plummeting through the earth, sirening and convulsing all the way down. Among the thousands, only Wally is put out—why destroy something so beautiful? The runaway daughter he's been tracking does this on repeat, again and again to the end of the projected world, which plays out in shapes, shadows and disappearing delusions, hyperbeams and history blasting to oblivion.

The hours pull Wally in every direction, until there is nothing left of him. He is a stranger in a sea of the estranged, sweating, taking stock of his wrongs here among the latest inheritors of Earth. But they move without a care, set free long ago in childhood by their dismal lot, sometime after the Long Heat, possibly before the oceans began truly to pulse.

In a rare moment of stillness, arriving like a safe day in an otherwise fire-torn season, Wally's blood buzzes. He sees it. A flash. The music opens itself up to him, and traces of what he can comprehend come through. House, shoegaze, grunge, dancehall, metal, soul, baroque pop, trap, vaudeville and burlesque, drum and bass. They are there and yet not. Each time he tries to connect all the sonic scrambles, meaning evades him.

Feeling its pull, he begins to let go, and somewhere in the passing mosh of futile, gyrating time, revelation floats above and before him—a colossal jade celestial orb, a planet kaleidoscoping through memories, passing from one geological era to the next in the space of songs. And then, at the very end, people and places. Their silly triumphs and tragedies, loves and losses, purchases and creations, playing out across the orb as it slides away into grey nothing, before finally vanishing.

Panic, cruel but just, sets in.

The thousands around Wally are in ecstasy. They cannot see it, he realises. It's for his eyes only, flickering in his vision, as he manipulates his sets, toggling it on and off. Jasmine knows he is here.

A voice comes to him lightly: *I'll be seeing you, Uncle.*

His vitals spike—the Reminiscence. He rushes back through the portal, stumbling into the main room and bar, which is mostly empty. Overawed, Wally wants to do it all over again. But for now, he'll wait for Jasmine.

'WHO YOU WAITING FOR, GEV?' Ignacio asks, as he serves a shivering Wally another kafo, warding off a bad nostalgia trip. 'You shouldn't take that stuff.'

'What the fuck do you know? You're barely old enough for memories.'

Ignació slots a rack of dirty bamboos into a dryer blade, blasting them. The place is emptying out, the procession of youth moving on to the next hot pulse, far off into the freezing night. 'That so, huh?'

'Yep,' Wally declares, rattled and downing the stimulant.

'I've lived enough,' Ignacio states flatly. 'And I'm zero-net to the core. I was just a kid when the first pulse hit Murcia. What do you have to show for your life, old man? Just sitting here dooming?'

Silence passes between them, suffocating.

Wally starts. 'Look. I'm sorry. Just a bit fucked up, that's all.'

'I can tell,' Ignacio says, crossing his glorious arms. 'So, like I said, who you waiting on?'

'Her,' Wally says, nodding over to the portal to the underground. He struggles to hide his soft centre.

Ignacio shrugs, vexed. 'How am I supposed to know who you're talking about?'

'The singer.'

'Jazmín?' he bellows, gushing in disbelief.

'That's right,' Wally says, nodding. 'She's my niece.'

Ignacio laughs uncontrollably, shrieking a little each time he thinks he's stopped. Wally finds it endearing.

'What?' Wally says, smiling.

'Nothing,' he says, innocently. 'You're just…something, aren't you?'

'I *am* her uncle. Sort of.'

'Sort of,' Ignacio scoffs, disbelieving. 'Well, you are old enough.'

They ease into a longer silence, orchestrated and delicate—a time-honoured pact between thinker and barkeeper, the pensive and the tender. Until it's closing time, and Wally has equilibrated.

Ignacio reaches out and places his hand on the older man's forearm, tapping his details. It barely leaves an impression upon Wally, desire having left him long ago, lost to a more colourful time.

Most things don't feel how they ought to anymore. With death prolonged, the edges that once defined life have come to lack definition. Often, Wally longs to return to the land of the living, but whenever he tries to ween himself off the longevity treatments, he cannot bring himself to do so. All he can do is obsess over the extra decades he has before him in which to fuck it up by some manner of unnatural cause. The natural will take him eventually, of course—a long time from now, when the world will be either made over or gone altogether. There is no cheating death in the end. And the game, it would appear for the millions of millennial Lifers, is to survive until that end—don't fuck it up yourself.

But for Wally, the worst part has been the guilt that racks his every waking moment.

He looks up at Ignacio, and, just as he's about to speak himself free, a voice comes lightly, this time closer. 'What are you doing here, Wal?'

AN EAGLE, she spreads her wings across the dilapidated corner booth, pecking flakes of pleather off its shoulder with the end of her fingernails. She gazes sidelong at Wally and beckons him, lashing out beneath the table at the opposite side of the booth with her talons, beneath which heavy black boots make a skeleton. He rushes over to her now. As he takes his place before her, she winds through the oddly tedious process of clearing her augmentations. The customisable skins dissolve about her—stunning fragments of light, vanishing into some extinction drive high in the heavens, safely off-planet.

Embodied augs have never been a feature of *The Chronicle*. These must be some kind of third-party nonsense, Wally guesses.

Anxious, he tries to express how glad he is to see her, blundering until he is cut off when Jasmine raises a flickering wing: '*Find.*'

The sound of her voice—syrupy, just like her mother's—soothes him, as though she were his own grown-up child.

'Huh?' he says, lost in her words.

'Don't you mean *find*? You're glad to *find* me, not see me.' The feathery features go out around her, many millions of disappearing miracles. As she watches them die, Wally detects a sadness slip over her. 'I didn't need finding, Wally. Just so you know.'

'I'm just here to see you, Jazzy. That's all.' Something quelled within him wants to break free; he keeps the feeling down with a splash of whisky. Jasmine orders some unrecognisable drink from Ignacio—'Ignay', she calls him—in an equally unrecognisable dialect.

They pass time between them, running through the years of each other's lives they've missed, their hearts counterpoised—one young and doomed and slurping poison, the other old and drinking away at the fountain of youth.

Jasmine lights up some unnameable object, like a bamboo obelisk hanging from her mouth, bubbling out wonderful smoke shapes.

'What the hell is that?' Wally begs.

'A smoke dolphin,' she says, giggling. 'I made these.' She puffs life into more animals and objects.

'No. I mean *that*,' he exclaims, pointing at her mouth.

'Oh. I call it a "Ka-Boomer." Designed this myself.'

'What's it for?'

'Nothing. Like most things. Just fun and a little kick.'

Ignacio sidles up to them to say goodnight. Before taking his leave, he tosses a set of keys to Jasmine, leaving the bar at her mercy.

'You're kind of a big deal around here,' Wally surmises, looking at her with curiosity.

She ignores him, offering only the faintest shrug. She bears a nonchalance he recognises, which he too bore as a young, unambitious musician. By all appearances, she gives exactly zero fucks; but Wally thinks he can make out something deeper going on beneath that front.

As the door slams and seals airtight behind Ignacio, Jasmine idly sings, 'He wants to fuck you.'

'I know. He tapped me.'

'Good for you.' She cracks a wry smile and spreads out across the booth. 'So, how'd you find me? I'm offnet…as much as I can be.'

'*The Chronicle.*'

'That thing? I barely used it, and when I did, it was all hacking.'

'I know. But facial recognition scraped your semblance.'

'Is that even legal?'

'Sort of. Depends. It's fine if no one finds out.'

'You realise how that sounds, right?'

'We don't spy—not really. And with billions of users, your parents wanted to see if you popped up. Raph's notching up a lot of hours these days, by the way.'

Jasmine tacitly ignores this last piece of information, filing it into the overflowing *who cares* category of modern life's effects. 'So you spied on me.'

Guilty, Wally sinks deeper into the booth. 'They just wanted to see how you are,' he explains.

Jasmine sits upright all of a sudden, back straight and arms crossed. And right there before him, she ceases to be little Jazzy. She is a different person. How long has it been since he last saw her? Six, seven years? He brings up the memory—her eighteenth birthday, surrounded by loving family and friends in a park, a sepia haze in the far distance, bushfire bleeding across the sky. Still early on, before Australia entered into the Pyrocene, entire years of fire.

She is adult beyond belief, now. It pains him, this corrupted passing of time, robbed of its natural nostalgia—of things moving at their sacred and right pace—as the world around him ages beyond recognition and will soon start to rush by him.

She grows serious quite out of nowhere and reaches out across the table, placing her hands over his. 'When did you start treating yourself?'

'A few years ago,' he admits, his shame faint but traceable by the corners of his unsteady eyes. 'How could you tell?'

She gazes into him, assessing—scanning, for all he knew—before sounding off: 'You don't look your age. You should look older.'

'Is that so?'

'Yes,' she says, nodding emphatically. 'You should be getting old about now. But I'm glad you're not. Not for the planet, just for myself.'

Wally cannot help laughing. It's like something she could have bluntly said years ago as a small, spirited child.

Although she doesn't know it, everything he has written during these collapsing decades—the novels, the interactives, the poetry, the scripts, the songs, the climate reportage, *The Chronicle* in its heyday—has been done with her in mind, to the best of his ability. For her and Raph. And for Benji, forever a baby.

She continues her enquiry. 'What about Mum and Dad? Have they…'

He shakes his head. 'They're not quite in the bracket. But they wouldn't anyway.'

'I dunno,' she says, doubtful. 'Your gen love to grab those extra decades, y'know, crying about all that your parents took from you.'

Wally finds this thoroughly amusing, before returning to the heart of the matter, shivering a little, averting his gaze. 'I know. I'm planning to stop.'

The moment passes. He looks up. She pities him, somehow.

'But you're not, are you?' she says. 'You can't possibly—I wouldn't. But I'll never have the chance.'

'I would give it to you, if I could.' He's heard rumours of how sick people can get if they take someone else's regimen.

She just nods—*sure, sure.* 'So, have you reserved a place in the towers or somewhere else fancy?'

Wally shakes his head, resolute. Against instinct, against the advice of certain highflying friends, he intends to stay grounded, continuing to fight.

'What will you do, then?'

'I'm going home for a while.'

'What, Canada?'

'Yeah.'

'You're barely Canadian anymore. Don't even sound it.'

He bobs his head around, fuzzy with the amalgam of colliding feelings. 'My mum's sick. I'm going to take care of her.'

'Margaret?'

He nods, keeping it together.

'I always liked her. I'm sorry to hear that.'

'She's not dead yet!'

'But she will be soon,' she states.

Her eyes, green and undisturbed as a forest in a better world, pierce him. There it is again, that childlike, unfiltered inflection, breaking him to smithereens, making him burst. And it all comes at once, flooding. 'I've—we've all missed you, Jazzy.'

She stands up swiftly and leans over the table, putting her forehead to his and clasping his thick mane with one hand, giving him permission to let it out. When she finally releases him, she jogs over to the bar and reaches for a bottle from the rack—something old—and pours them each another drink.

'Go home, Jazzy. Just for a visit. It's safer these days.'

No, she thinks, *it isn't*. 'It's an illusion,' Jasmine insists, hugging herself just enough to keep the world away. 'Everyone's been crushed into the cities, leaving the countryside to burn. No one really knows how bad it is. Cities will burn soon too. Or drown. Hey, maybe it will all happen at once and cancel itself out! I hear deniers and crims are onto that one now.'

Stricken, Wally looks at her, taking in the disunion of a family he has made his own for nearly half a crumbling century. It's hard to accept, his two families failing at the same time, echoing the world at large. It makes him want to go out the natural way, sooner rather than later. Endings abound, and yet his own is not certain.

'Sorry, Wal. I'm not going back.'

'*He* isn't there. Lives in New York these days, making big on posi-tive adaptation schemes. Real estate, hedge funds, public-private partnerships. Dumb bullshit like that. *But*—if you'll believe me—he has changed a lot from the little shit he used to be. As I said, he's a high-notcher and has become deeply concerned about things greater than himself.'

'I know,' Jasmine moans. 'I know more than you think. Doesn't change how I feel. Never will.' Her eyes flicker and flare with all the broken promises of the past.

How Raph had ridiculed her, made her a target at school, reducing her planetary fears to flashing content, recirculating in a very real world beyond parental reach, let alone comprehension.

Wally knows he should have stepped in. The development of *The Chronicle*, before it became a multimedia megahit, had kept him apprised of such rapid generational changes. He saw much of what happened coming. So, unlike Arne and Evie, it came as no surprise to Wally when Jasmine flew straight overseas after flunking school, disappearing to the best of her ability.

He nods. 'I assumed as much—that you knew some bits about Raph. Bright as you are.'

She rolls her eyes at this, but returns her gaze shortly, invested still, however vaguely, in avuncular praise, just as when she was tiny, dancing pirouettes, lullabying, running races and drawing pretty green worlds to unconditional applause. Some things endure.

'So, what did you think?' she asks eagerly.

'Of what?'

'The tunes, dickhead.'

The invective surprises him, an old Australianism breaking through her borderless, stateless voice. 'My honest opinion?'

She nods.

'I'm not sure. It was so intense. The sonics, the visuals, everything.'

'And?'

'And…I'd like to give it another try. I had a bad mix, though. I took some Reminiscence beforehand and it was overwhelming, for whatever reason. Still feeling it a little.'

'Oh, so *that's* why you're unbearably mushy.'

'Hey!'

'Whatever. We all need to get fucked up from time to time. Aren't you meant to keep that stuff locked up? You could sell your memories for a fortune around here. People will buy that trip.'

Wally waves his hand. 'Give me a break, officer. I'm travelling for a while. Needed the monthly doses on me. I got clearance.'

They grow familiar, remembering their old bond—how close they were.

Jasmine yawns, placing her hands down on the table and lowering her head to rest on them. Blurrily, she says, 'I'm glad you liked it, Uncle Wal.'

The ghosts of goodbyes seize them, icily from beyond the bar doors, the awful feeling that arrives on the verge of long farewells. Wally's mind turns apocalyptic and he wonders what in this age might take her—or him. An extreme weather event? An accident? Disease? He tries to tell himself that life finds a way, that it weathers all, that the planet isn't going to go out with a bang, some terminal punctum, and that he will see Jasmine again.

Unspoken, they shift in their seats, tarrying. Jasmine pours half a drink each. They toast to nothing.

'Do you still have the guitar?' Wally asks.

She bows, slow and tipsy. 'I have you to blame for my poverty.'

He cackles, conceding the truth of this.

They leave time to pass as it would, pausing only to turn over little leaves of the past—falling memories and how much every-thing has changed.

'Where will you go?' Wally probes.

Jasmine seems unwilling to speculate. Considering it, however, she says, 'Nowhere.'

'What?'

'I'll stay here. Until it gets too hard. And then I'll move on to the next thing. With the band, hopefully. We're doing a tour, actually. A real one.'

Wally shows his delight, trying hard to hide his concern. 'Where?'

She straightens up, drowning him in her stark gaze. 'Cold places.'

'I see. Well, it's great fun touring. Gruelling, though.'

'Why'd you stop playing? You were good.'

'I still play.'

'No, I mean properly. The Redcurrents. You guys were good. I've seen old YouTube vids.'

Wally sighs, mulling over a whole lifetime. 'It was a long time ago. I can't remember—I wanted to get clean, perhaps. I started writing more.'

'So that's it. Writing?'

'Yeah, maybe. You know how I was a climate reporter? I had a crisis—around your age or thereabouts—and wanted to work on something...*bigger*.'

'*The Chronicle*?' Jasmine enquires, a little sceptical.

Yes, he indicates. 'Though I didn't know it for another ten years or so. And now it's something else altogether, a well-staffed beast beyond my control. The board placate me, so long as whatever I want to do doesn't contravene international accords and quarterly projections. Don't worry'—Wally raises his hands—'I see the irony.'

'Good. Someone has to.'

'You don't rate it? You know, in spite of what it's become, it raised climate literacy to near universal levels. We built a bridge between data and emotion for billions of people.'

'Put it this way, I like your novels better,' she says, avoiding what she truly means: *But look what happened in the end!*

I tried, Wally wants to say. 'I haven't written a book in years, Jazzy,' he explains plaintively instead.

'You should.'

'I am.'

She stops, intrigued as she cocks her head, her dark curls, traced with a subtle yet wild array of colours he is only now noticing, dangling past her shoulder. 'What's it about?'

'It's a witness statement for the natural world. But it's also a letter—a long letter.'

'To?'

He pauses, searching for the right phrasing, even though he knows there is none. 'You,' he confesses.

'Me?'

Wally clarifies his meaning. 'Yes, you. And Raph. And Benji. All of you. All of you we robbed.'

Benji. She hardly blinks at the sound of the name of the brother she never knew. Wally cannot tell what it means to her. Nothing? Everything?

Jasmine metronomes back and forth in slow thought, until a look of approval comes over her. 'Well, I'll have to read that, then.'

'That would mean a lot to me.'

Yawning, Jasmine admits that it's time for her to scoot home for some sleep. Wally pretends he is in need of the same—he is departing early tomorrow. Melancholy guides them out the door, which Jasmine seals and locks, the cold hitting them like a physical object, comparable only to the Canadian winters Wally spent with his father, cabined up and going crazy late last century. He wonders what the ice will do to the people of this divine city, chief among them his niece, trotting beside him now, perhaps for the last time.

He offers to accompany her home, but she insists on guiding him back to his overnighter, he being a stranger in a desperate city. He accepts her help just as the extravagant arrival of midnight snowfall sweeps through. Along the way, he stumbles at various points; she knows the tricks of the pavement well and guides him along, holding him up.

They chuckle a little, whenever they get a moment to breathe, until they reach his stay, lamplit and of religious design, nestled deep in the old heart of the city. They both look on in wonder at the fragments of white swirling and descending around them. Nature bellows and they hold one another through the howl, as these two Weatheralls—a name, Wally realises in that moment, that is far more suited to Jasmine and her brave kind—farewell one another. And in that final embrace, Wally feels the strange transmigration of feeling, a certainty that love—not fear or anger or precarious circumstance, but *someone*—has kept her here. Wally leans back and, in the peaceful valley between question and claim, says: 'There's someone.'

There is, she nods.

12

TIPPING POINTS

Carbon dioxide parts per million: 614.5

The Earth tips, looking to overshoot.

In the vacuum of space, this little blue marble, streaked once with all the greens creatable, proceeds along its primordial ellipsis, going nowhere but deeper into the spiralling future, revolution by revolution, year by precious year.

And in a matter of only a few precious revolutions, the tipping is made clear. It is observed and recorded, verified, contested and confirmed, before being presented in unprecedented detail to the world. Although it need not be—eyes, at long last, would suffice—it is ironclad. An immense inertia has made its foretold return. Delicate systems, set off in the yesteryears of today's slowly dying men, start to teeter and shift, feeding back on one another, colliding in previously unimaginable ways.

Haunted, the children of the new world await what has been left to them. And they awaken.

THEY COME TOGETHER FOR A TIME, the briefest winter on record.

Evie settles into the old, rundown house with ease. They sleep together. In the afterglow, they gently remember why everything has happened as it has. A sense of survived parenthood passes through them, silent exchanges translatable only by two. To talk profusely would risk giving life to memories that cannot be endured.

But then, there is the burning desire to remember him, to breathe his tiny name into being.

In the unstoppable rush of events, as the largest ice shelf on Earth cracks way down below, Arne and Evie chirp, as empty nesters do, of children and why they are not here with them. They ring out, connecting to Raph occasionally, keeping an eye on all the changes, a topic their errant son avoids like a virus. As ever, Jasmine is harder to find, traces of her glimmering through the networked movements of friends and followers, winging through the final days of exotic places, singing the world anew.

The scenes come sliced, beamed through the vanilla ambience of official channels, as they peer, side by side, into the real core of happenings.

Wally plugs them into backchannels and withheld material. As Arne pours tea; as Evie reclines, sinking into old realisms no one heeded—Atwood, Bradley, Mitchell, Robinson; as they relearn the details of each other's bodies, governments topple and systems once thought inviolable collapse. Displaced millions fall out into ravening cavalcades, rolling across the Earth in search of their share.

One shivering evening, as they make a meal together sourced largely from the garden and windowsill, a pandemic reflex grips those parts of the world where freedoms continue to trump all else, people stocking up on every single thing from toilet paper to bullets, as if this were all temporary, as if this were something to wait out.

It all seems inevitable now as it unfolds before them. They pull each other close, at the end of each day.

On an unseasonal afternoon, cutting winter in half, Arne and Evie plod along the raised waterwalk bending along the bayside curves of the city, the new shorelines of suburbs they had wished to settle in decades ago. He lets her take his hand, the old warmth welcome even in the peculiar heat.

They shuffle across a side-bridge connecting to an island that used to be a hill, a beachside lookout people climbed in search of nothing so wonderful as a clear view, the horizon.

At the top, beneath the shelter of a wooden structure—a day-beacon, timeworn and flaking—a cold wind sings through, fading and final. Arne looks back at the mildly submerged playground structures peeking out through the surface of the water, where Raph and Jasmine and their friends used to play and party.

Leaning into one another, Arne and Evie combine thoughts. How they could have done more, somehow. Been more together, against the tide of greater events. They open up in ways that startle them both. They talk of Benji in a way they never have, calling him by name, wishing him a peaceful thirty-fourth birthday.

WAY UP IN THE FINAL CANOPY of a forest sentenced to death, a madman tormented by his own prolonged life rails against the machines and *lenhadores* raging below, in pursuit of final wood. Harbingers of death, they frighten and delight the mad professor, Thomas Hadley. He wants what they'll bring, but only for him— not for this now-impossible place, whose breath once filled the planet, whose rains gave succour to life's basin for many millions of years.

From his crowning perch, anointed and slippery with the centenarian's sweat, he conjures the past. The times he had been here, many years ago, in the blink of the forest's long life. To live to see something so old come to an end is like watching stars go out, the light leaving with them. He curses the longevity he has chosen. For it has truly begun—the Green Dieback, his life's nightmare, the undoing of all his work.

His chronicling eyes range the horizon. Currents of red and violet filter through, rising up into the sky—greenhouse gases as real-time data visuals. Fires rage in the real far distance, days away, ringing the scorched remnants of the planet's mightiest forest. He weeps for it and for the fight ending here, their arcs concluding together. His heart, like a great many things, changes: if longevity allows him to be here, cradling the green in its descent, holding it for a final, still moment, he is glad.

He looks out across the endless, ending distance. He unharnesses every part of his being. He leans out, digging his bootheels into this trusty kapok—*Sumaumeira*, the timeworn giant, guardian of Amazonia, making its final stand. They are here for one another. But still he keeps a primate limb wrapped around a young branch, holding on to old life.

Two hundred feet below, workers yell, '*Descer daí!*' They might as well speak the same tongue—*die!*—he muses. He sees their machines, lines them up. *No problem. Sem problemas.*

He lets go, passing through the canopy. Less startling, second time around, with purpose. He rotates and twirls, looking back up at the arboreal realm, tunnelling, all one wondrous primal green at this accelerating speed. It hums something his falling body finally grasps, here at the end. He draws in their breath and, in farewell freefall, echoes: *Survive*.

THE CHANGING WORLD weighs on John, an alien heat penetrating the ice of his hefty suit and pack. His armour against climbing temperatures, here in the desert that swells like ocean. He trudges along a gravelly ridge and up a rise before coming to painful standstill, lungs aching as he gazes down into the valley of nothing. The horror and the privilege of being here, even under surveillance.

He turns back to see Junfeng and his assistant, Haoyu, each struggling along the ridgeline, their gait twisting with terror. As they regroup, the late-afternoon sun breaks through the swirling towers of sand rising and shifting all around them. Like Mars, John surmises, but hot and inhospitable. The glare strikes the tinted plexiglass of their visors, reducing conversation to a crackling leap of faith.

'Down there! We can't go. But that's where it begins,' Haoyu yells over comms, unaware of how loud he is in John's ear.

'And where it ends,' John fires back, his wit not lost on Haoyu. But Junfeng, withered and aged by the unliveable heat and aeolian

forces that have decimated much of inland China, remains
unmoved.

There was once a common misconception that a life of
observation might steel a person for the planet's unravelling;
overwhelmingly, the opposite is turning out to be true. Archival
evidence of this is everywhere, journals given over to jeremiads,
grammars of grief evolving down the years. For John, this kind
of stealthy denialism that pervaded early twenty-first-century
thought—the delusion that knowledge provides distance, that
solutions would arrive *somehow*, so inexorable was the march
of progress—was and remains an egregious fallacy. History is
characterised by occlusion, the masking of truth by the powerful;
an unwriting. And John feels the unwriting of people and their
land in the Tipping—the voiceless millions starving and fleeing—in
ways few could understand. But the truth always remains, waiting
to be unearthed.

'Will it stop?' John asks, gesturing towards the wasteland below,
marked by sand-drowned abandoned structures.

Haoyu and Junfeng exchange an uneasy look, before the
younger man—Haoyu—explains that no one knows for sure,
that the expanding desert sea bears traces of a boundless, runaway
effect. Half-knowing the answer already, John asks about the
millions who called this region home.

An uneasy silence passes between the three of them, before
Junfeng speaks at last: 'They are taken care of.'

John shudders a little in the artificial cool of his suit; he senses
the same monitored unease in his companions, thinking of all
the dead below.

'We must go now,' Haoyu indicates, pointing towards the sand-
storm, an ochre wave unfurling slow and mighty on the horizon.

The window to get back to the research station is closing, as
is John's mind. It's a short descent back down to their transport,
but Junfeng, if the ascent was anything to go by, will require a
safe margin.

'Those buildings down there—they are old posts, right? There are provisions? Solar?'

. John makes out Haoyu's apprehension even through the increasing crackle of their comms: 'Yeah…'

'Okay. You get the professor back to base. I'm going to push on.' John sees the terror on their faces, clear through the dust and tint of their visors.

'You cannot go down there,' Haoyu insists. 'You are not allowed.'

'I can.'

Haoyu lunges forward, reaching out to grab John before he is blocked suddenly by Junfeng's outstretched arm. Shocked, the young man looks back at his superior, protesting in rapid Mandarin before Junfeng reverts to English, explaining calmly, 'Let the man go.'

The silence is deafening, the wind swirling the dust around them. John nods with respect to Junfeng. 'Will you two be okay?'

'We should be able to make it back,' Haoyu estimates, still panicked, and running the numbers rapidly through his head. 'Maybe with an hour or two to sp—'

'He doesn't mean that.' Junfeng looks directly at John with what he could only be described as affection. The old man reaches behind his ear and flicks their comms to a closed network. 'Remember,' he begins, 'we lost long-range comms in the storm. You lost your mind'—he points in mock accusation at John. 'You ran off. We could not stop you.'

'Thank you,' John says. The two of them exchange looks of aged mischief, while Haoyu, a model research assistant, contorts through the calculus of career sabotage, sentencing a man to death and making it back home safe.

'We should all get moving,' Junfeng states with a calm that John could do with right now. 'Good luck, John.'

As they wonder off down the rise, their silhouettes fade into dust, disappearing. He looks down into the valley of the dead. It isn't far to the first outpost—he gives himself a fifty-fifty chance of making it—towards which he geomarks a path as he switches on his bodycam.

He will raise truth out of the ground and into the world.

ALONG A ROAD MADE FOR NEW FORTUNE, running deep into the northwest, further than previously possible, the same drifts that once bore snow now bear the leaflitter of a juvenile, mischievous afforest, about which moose snuffle and grunt, lapping from the Arctic meltwater flowing into the outlandish, shifting river systems with which language has yet to catch up. Dangerous, budding sublime. Brief beauty on a broken continent.

Wally shifts gears and takes the old road—once the only road—towards memories mixed and frozen.

He has driven all the way across Canada, through adapted cities and forgotten, abandoned towns. New farming zones and hydrocollectives of the north, a frontier both expanding and retreating. After four days and two nights of quiet at the wheel, listening to classics by the letter—Powers, Proulx, Proust—he entered the northwest beneath the dark, tumbling universe, indifferent to his cause, with little but a truckful of his mother's possessions.

He pulls up at the large double gate, still intact somehow, as wide and proud as the redwood from which it came. The moon winks out and releases the sun, lighting up the past and revealing the present. At the threshold of the old family homestead, Wally feels home at last.

And yet not.

Decades on, the morning light plays differently here, sweeping low through the woodland, quivering green, flickering gold and crimson in strange arrays. Stunning. It won't last, he knows. The boreal forest dieback has begun. He imbibes the change, memorialises it for the colourless age to come.

Once, in Wally's long-ago, this place used to freeze over and take time with it. Closed off for months at a stretch from the great acceleration of life. His father would bring him here to give living a pause. He sees that man—philosopher, scholar, public intellectual—in a different light now, of course, but his handiwork and temperament are carved and shot into every nook and cranny of the property. Wally strolls down a thousand moments and up towards the porch, timeworn and desolate.

He halts. Forever young, he crouches on the steps for a while, breathing in the endless change, the expanding green in place of white. How many days had he perched right here, bored beyond repair, waiting for something—anything—to happen? The place never moved; now it moves too fast.

Looking out, he tries for a different image, and it startles him what deviceless, unaided memory can do. His mind draws up a remarkable world of snow. Mounds like mountains to a child, collapsing underfoot and refreshing in the rapid flurry, over and over in an ageless cycle, rising and falling on end.

He holds it for a minute, ignoring the thawing present—iceless, save for some wintry miracle or apparition of his own design. He's too tired to conjure such things this morning. The white of the past drifts away. His spirit is dampened as he rises to enter the large logwood cabin of cleaved spruce and cedar, untended for many years but for the council of trembling aspen, overseers of this melting world, encircling this home.

He knows better. He knows they are one, the aspen. A colony of clones, gold and glorious. Their bare, self-pruning trunks, waving ramets to one great organism, one parental root system—all interconnected. Their eternal agreement and unity, unlike anything in walking history. What secrets they might trade in the underland. Do they sense his newfound appreciation and awe? Do they know what is coming?

Some peace and acceptance visit Wally; their quietude fills his lungs.

He opens the door and enters the elaborate space within, dust-streaked and cobwebbed but surprisingly orderly. It's still too cold up here to squat, and with the population rolling into neighbouring new zones—allotments for final farming and ferming experiments—looters seem to have been warned off. For now.

It is as it was, the undeniable power of time and memory both steadying him and shaking him. The mahogany piano, woefully out of tune but sonorous as ever; his father's arsenal, unrifled; the cast-iron fireplace, so oddly lonely, abandoned. He would put it to use in a matter of hours.

He gets to settling in, lugging a little of his life—instruments, provisions and whisky, old books, his interface, tablets and an unregistered MacBook from decades ago for writing—along with every essence of his mother into that space, burdening it with love and loss.

Tomorrow morning, he will wake up, make coffee and maple-soak some expired oats, gaze emptily out the grimy window—the one facing onto the aspen, the rising river beyond—before moving over to his father's desk, an alcove of ingenious arrangement, and begin to write for the last time, starting with two words: *Dear Benji.*

IT IS NEVER TOO LATE to admit you were wrong. That's the message Raph takes with him when he signs out. It rings over and over in his head, deafening and heavy, a worldly weight crushing his chest. He swipes away New York State's denier's anonymous portal—his seventh session now—and decides, for the first time in weeks, to take a walk for no reason other than that his world is collapsing. Weeks of change, both within and without, have sent Raph spiralling; but strange new voices overflow, taking the place of the old.

Keyboard warriors, friends. Every voice, not his.

How they swirled and danced thrillingly before him in the old web, a primitive place. The temptation to dive back in is very real. An hour or so running through some *Chronicle* modules will get him through the night. Shame swarms around him on both sides. He is a traitor, either way. And lonelier than ever today, strolling down Lower Manhattan, taking Broadway in the everfall, sure signs of the winter to come. Resolute, he turns on his umbrella and strikes out for Battery Park, drowned and down by the river.

He is heading for the wall. Just one last look, before he checks into a new worldview.

Twenty minutes of dreaming later, and with his heartrate elevating to between 97 and 123 beats per minute, Raph steps into the squelch. His feet cannot lie, but he still draws up the latest PalimpSet overlay and looks back through the centuries: towers rising and falling, people coming and going, the Earth changing rapidly. He permits the voiceover and recognises it immediately: Uncle John. The gruff timbre and weary lilt set Raph aflame with the heat of younger days. Like many expatriates, he hasn't set foot in Australia for over a decade. Regret swirls around him. He is no climate criminal. He has always abided by the law, keeping his errant second life concealed.

He listens to the old philosopher as he makes his way to where the expanding Hudson flows out toward Staten Island and beyond. At the edge of the park, he stands by one of the benches, stalling, noticing the very moment the old lampposts come alive in the fading afternoon. The everfall begins to ease. He stands still through time immemorial, according to John.

As the voice rolls on, Raph switches off and takes the many clunking steps up the newly raised wall—a brutalist, iron and compounded tragedy, imposing itself on his will. The automatic gate to the walkway along the top of the wall is open today, the forecast favourable. He craves a vista, even a grim horizon.

Across the water, Staten Island's wall remains half-raised, the upshot of the latest revolution, the refugees of forgotten Pacific islands refusing the torrid conditions of their labour that previous summer. In a panic, waterfrontage right across New York either sold or boarded up fast. The tension is rising still in the great city, shifting in the immense tide of onrushing time.

He switches views, between what once was and what now is, with extraordinary clarity. He knows; he has always known, but his reasoning was elsewhere, off after his mother searching for a mirage he came to hate, off in spaces that replaced his empty husk of a father. He remembers the green grief of his high school years, so utterly without future, and how he turned away and found safety, nestled in the backrooms and man caves of the reactionary, typing into oblivion.

But his sister—how he misses her. Every hour of every day, if he were to be true to himself. Where is she? Is she safe? Is she happy? Once, he could have reached out, but now whenever he thinks about doing so his spirit fades. Her silence—her offlining—is sign enough.

As he laments, some uncanny voice rises through him. At the same time, strands of light—precious, sacred sunlight—break out through the cloud cover, coruscating down to the river, near where it flows into the Atlantic. Luminous accompaniment. Raph toggles views, checking that it's real.

Hello, Raphael, comes the voice, this time clearly.

'Hello,' Raph replies, taking his breath beat by broken beat. Waves crash against the wall. The city darkens around the light.

How are you today?

'I'm alright.'

You don't sound well, nephew.

'Uncle Wal?'

Indeed.

'You spying on me through your sick little game?'

I wouldn't call it a game—though there is the interactive media hub. Award-winning, that department keeps telling me. I see you've finished all the narratives. And by the looks of things, you've platinumed many of them. Don't worry, there'll be more soon. Though I'm not involved anymore, so they will lack a delicate touch. I'm away… writing something else.

'Cool story, Uncle. Is this even legal? Can you just communicate with everyone like this?'

No. Just you. Special favour for your parents. And a few select others, of course. Surprised you didn't detect the glitch in your set. Some coder you are!

Raph stands there, indifferent to the sea spray battering him. He pulls his parka tight to his body and raises its hood. 'What do you want?'

I'm just checking in on you, buddy.

'Sure you are.'

There's a silence between them, humming across thousands of miles. Until Wally breaks it: *Don't be like that. You know, I've always thought of you as a son, Raph.*

'No! Tell me—why now all of a sudden?'

Raph can't see Wally, but he can hear the discomfiture in his silence, wherever in the world he might be.

Things are changing, Raph. If you go into some of the modules, you'll see some tipping points, chain reactions, many think have begun.

'Think?' Raph scoffs, waving Wally away.

You can't wave me away like that.

'You can see me? What the fuck! I could report all this.'

I can wipe all this right now.

'Go ahead.' He hears Wally sighing—fondly, if he's not mistaken.

You always were a little shit.

'Guilty.' They share a laugh. 'How are you, then, Uncle?'

Oh, you know, just working through a lifetime of regret. The things we—I—could have done differently for you. All of you. And I'm working out how to apologise for that, now.

'You can't.'

Oh, so you're listening to the science now?

Raph starts to choke up. 'Wal—'

I'm sorry. I didn't mean it like that.

'It's fine. I deserve that.'

So. How are you really, then?

'Oh, you know, just working through a lifetime of regret.'

He can hear his uncle smiling. *Very good. Can we do this more? Talk like this.*

'That'd be good. But like I said, what's the sudden rush?'

I worry.

'These tipping points?'

Yes. Those and many other things.

Raph brings up an information panel in his view and scrolls. 'You say "many think"—they don't know for sure? Sounds speculative.'

Careful, buddy. You could get arrested in some places for such talk.

'Just some healthy scepticism.'

Don't fool yourself. I wouldn't call it that.

'The science should be certain.'

Well, it is, in a sense. And that's not how it works, Raph. You can't know everything. We are the unpredictable part—the true variable. What we do or don't do determines what will happen. Humankind, try as we might, is notoriously hard to predict.

The notion makes Raph uncomfortable—that the whole thing is out of control. It would be better if we were just wrong all along. He remembers his training and resists the thought.

'Okay…well, what can we do?'

Raph—Wally's voice frightens him now—*listen to me. Reach out to the ones I know you love most—your family. I have to go now, but I have a message for you. From your uncle.*

'Freddie? I don't want to have anything to do with that terrorist.'

Just listen to him, please. It will autoplay when I leave. It's encrypted to your retinal profile, so you're safe. Okay?

He's uncomfortable but agrees, more out of curiosity than anything else.

See you round, Raph.

'See you round, Uncle Wally.'

The transmission dies and Raph is left alone for a few unmediated seconds. His view is crystal clear even as the darkness arrives. And then suddenly a pre-recorded Fredric Bakke shimmers into view, muscular and alarmingly gentle, leaning forward from a wooden stool in an empty room fit for interrogation.

Hello, Raphael. Nephew. According to my intel, you have never parted ways with something I gave you many years ago. You've kept it safe. Good. The time has come for you to use the token—the badge—I left you and your sister. Upload its data to your interface—I trust, with your expertise, that you'll know how to use a secure channel. I have an offer for you, which you may take or leave.

Freddie falls silent, rubbing his afternoon stubble, brooding. Raph looks more closely and sees the grey of his age. The man, against all vanity, had resisted longevity treatments. He could easily have accessed the black-market stuff and yet evidently had not.

This mortal man—capable of great violence, it is said—concludes: *See you round, kid.*

Everything before him disintegrates, leaving him to a dark reality. Raph is hungry all of a sudden and scrolls for some nearby takeout. Before getting down from the wall, he moves to the rail edge, taking one last look. Another pulse is coming in a few months—a chunk of West Antarctica—and access to the wall will be restricted.

He sprays code into the air over the precipice, hoping some love might take and not bite back.

SOMETHING LIKE POWER courses through Kim for a moment. From on high, she oversees the many hundreds below, anting across the old, abandoned hangar, readying to ship out and change the world. But even now, after years in shadow, she wavers. As Freddie rallies more to their cause, the direction of which strays evermore into uncharted territory, something gnaws at Kim.

Freddie departed with the same missionary certainty he always did, leaving Kim and the top grass to organise and mobilise while he hunted and gathered—this time with a specific, familial target in mind.

She retreats into the dim shell of their headquarters. She slumps back in the old office chair, a throwback to her doctoral days a lifetime ago, and raises her boots up onto the grossly oversized and militarised desk. In stillness, she is helpless to thought. It has been consuming her more and more of late. The urge to run, to guide Freddie in a different direction—*No, fuck that, to overthrow Freddie*. Her pulse is racing through the moment, the execution of which comes to her in dreams more than waking. And then it's gone, just like that. She breathes through the ache.

Humanity is slipping, and it isn't here where she always imagined it would be. She feels the urge to march out and command all the people below to flee while they still can, to go home to their families. And then she remembers how many of them have lost everything, how vulnerable they are. Everyone here has lost something. Where Freddie has long instructed them in how to take back the world, Kim finds now that she wants nothing more than for them—for *all* the world—to avoid as much loss as possible. Although a realist, she still knows how to dream, how to hatch her own plans.

She shifts in her chair, reaches over and snaps the blinds up. Light, clear and crepuscular, breaks into the quarters. Motes of dust surf silently on its yellow glow. She reaches out childlike and tries to catch some. Minutes go by and the temptation to make contact overwhelms her. She tilts her head towards the window, to the chop of the ocean, to the sound of gulls fighting along this abandoned stretch of coastline. She could call Evie. Or Arne. Old ways, an old life beckoning her to return. She could warn them that Freddie, instead of admitting how he longs for family, has become hellbent on recruiting his unrecruitable nephew, Raph, the sweet child she once knew—decades ago, before disappearing underground. She hopes he resists, remains immune to Freddie's magnet.

She could call John.

World-weary, she lowers her head onto the desk, watching the chop of the ocean, falling into dreams.

IN THE UPPER STOREY of a crumbling house in an aquavillage in a part of the world new to her, Jasmine catches strands of confusion from the other side of the planet, faint bits of brotherly code begging to be answered. She scrolls through the message and pauses, only for a moment, before moving on with her life, filled as it is now, if not with hope, then with love. There is singing, a harmony, echoing across the new tide. She leans out the window, bracing her hands against the cool stone wall and makes them out in the glimmering distance, rowing a gondola's worth of necessities home.

WE SHOOT OVER THE EDGE.

At first it stuns the world, until it doesn't anymore. In hindsight, it comes to seem obvious, inevitable. The planet gives over to catastrophic flux. Systems unravel at a speed and scale beyond reckoning.

Forests, the largest of lungs, rot and die; polar ice continues its cold farewell; depleted oceans, turning acidic, refuse to absorb the excesses of human progress; deep formations, the ancient and patient currents of the oceans, stall and redirect, giving rise to strange new climes; sea levels and deserts rise together, channelling populations from both the heart and the edge of continents onto reformed coastlands. The first inhospitable zones of the Earth are drawn, swelling out and forcing an unliveable number into forlorn cavalcades, marching to places that will not take their kind—things close off, people fall back and retreat. Isolate. And in only a matter of years, humanity becomes hard to find.

And yet many places hold out. Some hardly change at all. The distribution of effects is uneven, unpredictable. And somehow, as throughout history, the rich and fortunate and powerful find safe purchase in the tipping tree of life.

But the brave new children of this world are awakening. Futureless, with their eyes on the past, they know where to look.

CENTURY'S END

13

THE DRIFTER

Carbon dioxide parts per million: 626.8

Down.
Down.
Down.

Down into the dark. Further than ever before. Beyond the light of stars, where blue gives way to black.

Trencher-9 drifts with the undercurrent winds, descending into that perpetual darkness, where even the faintest blue tendrils of sunlight cannot penetrate, disappearing kilometres ago, away into twilight. Midnight water. The capacitive red light of the cabin flickers and signals: *life.* Oceanic residents of the abyss, neon and translucent and ductile. Far from alien, there is nothing so earthly in this world. Their soft kind have wimpled and foraged along the deepest surfaces of the planet since before biology managed to walk and breathe air.

The monitors feedback aquatic clicks and creaks and gushes, benthic chatter. And Evie, nuzzled within the cockpit, leaning in to those signals, seeking ways to shapeshift and leave the burning world of humans behind, is peaceful in that abyss. Floating. No need to comprehend it fully; just to be in its impossible midst is a bottomless freedom far greater even than that which years of free-diving have given her.

Fathoms down, she kicks in the reverse-thrusters, stabilising and monitoring the pressure systems and cabin integrity. This is her twelfth voyage, yet she still trembles with terrified delight at the eerie marine world within reach, separated only by glass and metal and ingenuity. The immense pressures down here would compress her hoary body to death in moments. She fantasises about it—ghoulishly, she knows.

She diverts power to the front and rear rotary orbs and casts this deepest of ocean trenches aglow. The sedimentary rocks here, coated in mats of bacteria, have never known such wavelengths. They seem to flinch, before shimmering with new knowledge.

Sorry. But Evie cannot resist. She has to see what is down here.

Her team had approval for only six dives this moon, with a clear and specific mandate: maintenance and retrieval. Permission to observe and survey marine life on an incidental basis—one of Evie's preconditions—was granted informally, such was the demand for her specific skill set.

She clings to the idea that down here she'll discover something new, or some leftover thing that has simply been hiding in the deep for decades, healing. A shark. A blue whale. She rubs her icicle hands together, warming them: *Don't hold your breath.*

Evie sweeps along the ocean floor. She makes out prawn-like amphipods and bottom-feeding sea cucumbers. Grenadier skimming the seabed just above spoonworms that slink along, churning up deeply bedded sand, billowing gently on the slowest seconds imaginable, the speed of deep water, before falling back down, stringy and cumulous.

Hours like minutes drift by. And then, without warning, the drifter known as *Trencher-9* stalls, coming to a complete and unremarkable halt, its lighting systems crashing as it drops those final metres to the seafloor in impossible darkness, falling into bed and eternal slumber.

Far from being panicked, Evie suspects this might be what she has been wishing for all along, in taking the drifter for absurdly expensive, unlogged joyrides. She is more amused than anything else. Her indiscretions will turn up in corporate accounts, no doubt. But by then she will have provided them with what they want. Or she'll be down here for the rest of time. Irretrievably lost, though eventually found. All manner of creatures would adorn this coffined vessel, life coming to nest there in its various mechanical alcoves along with rich bacteria and colonies of algae. Whole eras would pass, empires rise and fall, continents shift and resettle, species evolve and vanish from here. How long her bones, sepulchred there in the near-freezing depths, might endure.

Her pulse finally rises. And human fear, so basic—so essential—kicks in. It courses from within and sharpens everything from without.

She fumbles around on the console before her, brailing along the complex grid of keys and switches until she locates the largest and most pronounced toggle, restoring backup power. It works—powering oxygen, voice command, interior lighting and vital cabin functions. She calls up the drifter manual to the console touchscreen, deciphering its table of contents and manically scrolling through hundreds of pages. Down, down, down. Forever it goes.

Who the fuck wrote this?

Sweat pools in her jumpsuit. It drips off her. Salty rivulets trickle down to the bottom of the screen, falling there to the steel floor. It patters a tinny pulse, droplets landing at half the rate of her heartbeat but rising, cascading. Soon they synchronise.

Everything is rising, except *Trencher-9*.

She manages to locate the mechanical reboot section, steadies herself and methodically follows the steps. She waits wild-eyed and heaving, as the metal beast whirrs and runs through various sequences. Minutes pass forever. They could be her last; they could be her first. First in a new life, yes.

She kisses the necklace Raph made for her as a boy, runs its wooden charm across her teeth. She wonders what Jasmine is up to, wherever in the dangerous world she is right now. And Arne. Yes. When she gets back to the surface, she will find him. It has been too long. She wants to scream, but instead is overcome by crying and painful laughter.

In her agonising wait, she becomes lost to silence. She builds enough strength to yell, viscerally and from the depths of her diaphragm. The noise like the lion-roars she used to perform, prowling on all fours for Raph and Jazz when they were little, echoes metallically around the compartment.

Trencher-9 begins to quake, cowering in its death throes. Drones and clankings drive up and up, increasing in pitch and urgency but faltering over and over, clogging terminally at the critical moment before winding down in failure.

Evie swivels around to face out the window, before her like a sheet of obsidian rock, cold and devoid of light. She could divert some precious power to the orbs, light up the world again. But she waits, helpless.

She closes her eyes and, as always, Benji comes to her. What he would look like. Who he might be. She can hardly recall the chubby crevices of his cherubic body anymore. He rises and falls in her mind every day, never still enough to recognise.

But now, with only hours of oxygen remaining, at the bottom of the western Pacific Ocean, she feels closer to him than ever. She could let go, drift off, reach out and swaddle her boy once more.

She closes her eyes.

EVIE WAKES TO A GREAT CLAMOUR, a life-affirming turbulence that throws her from her seat. She falls hard but barely registers the pain. The drifter has clunked back to life and is coasting along its earlier course, like nothing ever happened. As if nothing went terrifyingly awry.

'You cunt,' Evie chants, manic and elated. 'You beautiful cunt.'

She climbs up into her seat and takes control. While *Trencher-9* equilibrates, Evie's body runs awash with great clusters of chemical ensigns, hormones and neurotransmitters discharging, colliding—a little big bang. Primordial, a beginning. She could have drifted off, but here she is, now, alive.

Evie is rising. Up.

Up.

Up.

Up.

And, with eerie routine, she proceeds along the original trajectory toward the carbon sequestration purlieu, where various emission-sinking experiments are carried out.

There's a lot of money in saving the world. A whole economy, conglomerates of history's great polluters, pivoting, pledging and thriving. Innovations. Solutions. Shoppers, exalt—no need to revolt. The planet has been put out to tender! And look, here is the ocean. Blue as it ever was, just how your grandparents remember it. We came from there. It will take our plumes of excess, dispatched along pipes. It's already doing the bulk of the work anyway, has done so throughout time, right back to the Cambrian, eons ago.

Evie shudders. Of course this was the greatest vision they could manage: behemoth phalluses plunging into the ocean, ejaculating and thereby coming to save the world.

She comes around now in a sweeping manoeuvre, piloting through complex rock formations, jagged aquatic mountainsides, and crossing the threshold into the sequestration purlieu, a dense and acidic carbon lake saddling the ocean floor. Myriad carbon hydrates, chunks like large cuts of igloo ice, float and fall in the vastness. Great tunnels of downward pipe eject humanity's favourite chemical compound and emission of choice.

She chugs safely beneath them and, rotating the orbs, casts the littered world below in glorious white light.

She descends.

She engages upward thrusters, coming to a hover over a perfect pile of six-month-old hydrates—not too densely packed, just enough to hold together and not tumble.

Evie inserts the extraction mechanism—an arcade-like but highly dexterous claw—and on first attempt grabs hold of a perfect block, glistening and ominous, a stable form teeming inside with a little monstrous everyday history. Boring and apocalyptic. She smoothly retracts the mechanism and buckets the sample into one of *Trencher-9*'s containers.

She has been tasked during her contract with collecting various samples, each exposed to deep sea conditions for various amounts of time, to test their viability as carbon sinks. And she's damn good at this game—her benevolent and budget-cutting overlords nearly lost one of their best players today. When she gets back to the rig, she'll have to log *Trencher-9*'s deadly malfunction with the robots in maintenance.

She'll need to start ascending soon, but there's enough oxygen for a dance.

Diverting extra power to the front orbs, she glides forward, lacing gracefully from pipe to pipe, their waste slipping by her side as she pitches and yaws perfectly. At the edge of the purlieu she catches a shadow in the depths below, slipping across her lights some hundred metres away. She veers towards the shape, twisting and flailing in an alarming spasm.

Closing in, Evie rotates the front orbs across its shifting vector and catches a set of panicked eyes, globular and ancient grey. A fish, large and with no human name. She does not know it—although it seems to know her, recoiling as it is approached by *Trencher-9*.

'What's wrong, buddy,' Evie sings, reaching out and placing a palm against the glass. 'What's your name?'

It continues to thrash. Why has it not fled? She leans in, peers even closer.

And then she sees it.

The fish is trapped. It writhes, twisting to break its flesh free. It is coming apart. Its body, sheeny and vermicular in those final moments, sheers with the force of its own long and desperate struggle.

Evie screams. She jumps away in fright, reeling, seething. Eventually, she manages to return to the window. In the stillness, she identifies the pliable but unbreakable substance, still tangled around the remaining front half of the fish: plastic. Unimaginably far from where it came. The ocean, retaining what humankind has tried to forget. That old abandoned and terribly everlasting thing, haunting them still.

Ubiquitous micro-bits of it seeping into the Earth and every living thing. Larger, catchable portions of the stuff rolling in the wind across the surface of the world, through cities sinking and otherwise, expanding towns, and the diminishing, overpopulating ribbons of land between. Colourful islets of this strange matter, brought together on currents great enough to be named, forming ramshackle seasteads, extraordinary waterworld hamlets, junk-island nations, brave homes for the displaced and dispatched who insist on living.

Evie shifts in her seat, suddenly lonely. In the deep ocean murk, clarity comes to her unbidden. Some sober alien, krakening away inside, whispering clearly. *You nearly died. Look how this poor, wonderful fish tore itself in two. Go home. Leave this dead place of vain experiments. Go home.*

Evie focuses. She brings the drifter up in a steadily rising sequence, proceeding cautiously through the gauntlet of hope-laden penis pipes, each trickily coming into view only once in range of *Trencher-9*'s light beams. Far greater in diameter than the failing composite shell around her, they always look as though they might shuck her out and shoot her up into them. If she were to venture too close.

Hours pass. As she reaches the surface water, rippling through sun-stroked shallows, Evie starts to say her goodbyes to *Trencher-9*. On approach to the rig, she collects her photos and talismans, trinkets made by small hands long ago, adorning the console. She docks the drifter, logs the cut of hardened carbon, unlocks the top hatch and speedily disembarks, stepping into a world of blistering heat. She unzips her jumpsuit, opens it up to dangle from her hips, dank with the sweat of death.

She looks around. No one here registers her safe return. They rush about the platform doing sundry tasks, sweating and swearing—cursing their world. Would she have sent out a distress call at the last? Probably. Then again, maybe not.

She says farewell to the ocean. Exhausted, she knows it will save nothing and that she cannot save it. She apologises for abandoning it—big blue, lovely and dying, with glistening crests of cream, all the way to the horizon in every direction. She breathes in a lungful of it, before rushing to her berth to contact someone far away.

14

MELTWATER

Carbon dioxide parts per million: 632

In the ending years, as wonder gives way to grief, old friends take one last holiday together to make an unfathomable farewell.

The journey poleward aboard the new-gen ship *Solaris* has made for an unnerving passage, a strange three-day odyssey from Ushuaia, Argentina, wind-ravaged and recovering from red tides, to Antarctica, where, as if carbon could time-travel, ice once thought permanent and impenetrable now buckles beneath the forces of the past. The few hundred souls aboard the silent ship share the same lonely apprehension, laced with a hope so unfounded as to make planetary pilgrims of them all.

Arne wanders across the deck to Evie, by the railing since first light, her gloved hands sliding back and forth in pale bewilderment at the dying mystery before her. She breathes in the entire horizon, all the while recording what she can for safekeeping. He places a puffy glove in hers and she shifts across, bumping up together, shouldering one another with warmth and weight and shared time.

Wally and John, still mischievous together decades on, push through a long night of carousing below deck to brave the cold and join the Bakke-Weatheralls up top as the *Solaris* nudges through a flotilla of icebergs, missives from Antarctica's collapsing west.

Soon enough, the deck begins to overflow with the murmuring movements of pilgrims, toggling views, Wally realises, between what is and what was, and what could have been. Some advancement on his original masterpiece, he supposes; he's given up on keeping up with it. A nearby group of pious wanderers—Creation's Carers, Wally presumes, by the looks of them—set about singing some hymn to the world of white they will soon need to figure out how to live without. It stirs him a little, though he cannot quite say why. Melody, he rationalises.

Disturbed, even from this distance, John shakes his scruffy head, reeling off a litany of *told you sos*. He had also ventured to the Arctic for the final watch, when the last great glaciers cracked and collapsed, sending out immense waves of icebergs on doomed wakes, the methane and hydrocarbons gushing out of the region for all the world to see and chronicle through new dimensions of global perception. And here John is, on the other side of the world, waiting to be proven right yet again, as if it were ever in doubt, etched at length across the course of events.

In remorse, the four friends move closer to one other. The *Solaris* glides ahead, the collapsing continent stretching on endlessly. Seizure has taken its mystery.

The night before, the captain explained in passing to Arne how he always sails through the Ring of Rigs at night, running the course of the continent where the first developments were making new ground, rising up. A wizened man of generous spirit, not unlike Arne's famously deceased supervisor Thomas Hadley, he'd leaned in conspiratorially to explain that this was 'to maintain the dream'.

Arne shudders. There is nothing dreamlike here. He turns to Evie and, after such long companionship, senses the breaking. By touch, he knows it. She thought it might call to her somehow, this place and its past complex of life, but it does not, overrun as it is by the interests of humans. She hasn't even bothered to unpack her equipment today, so impossible is the thing she seeks nowadays.

Drifting towards its designated dock, situated on one of the better preserved sections of West Antarctica, the *Solaris* whirrs with something like distress, some noise that should not be here.

And the four friends feel a strange complicity in the emerging reality onto which they are about to step.

'We shouldn't be here,' Evie says, low.

The others sense it also—the trespass, the treason of this disaster tourism, as with the reef half a century ago.

Evie and Arne form a tight embrace, remembering—feeling— every shared fragment of their lives in the span of just seconds. Wally and John join in, forming a second circle of arms around them, a silver lining. Against ruin, they laugh with an unbreakable love many hundreds of years old stacked together.

They disembark, stepping out into the place where beauty and fragility meet as nowhere else on Earth. Even now, terraformed beyond repair, every surface of the ancient continent crackles with an indefinable energy, an otherworldliness. The clouds above seem to travel over the still continent at astonishing speeds today.

They haul themselves up to a newly laid track slithering inland, inset for miles on end with the trademark that has brought this experience to you. Unnerved after only a few hundred metres, they scuffle off-track and decide to explore a nearby segment of exposed coastline.

Fitter than his biological years, Wally leads the way, testing the ground ahead of his ailing friends. To his surprise, Evie outmatches them all for endurance, striking out cleanly towards the end of the world.

After an hour or so, the pearly white spread they arrived at begins to slip away, revealing a muddying expanse of hummocks out of which tufts of green shoot, looking to live. They struggle through the sludge, holding each other up.

Not long after they clear the sleety bog, a thrumming comes to them from nearby, building rapidly to a crescendo. The wind rises above the ice-shattering thump. Soon, pools of blue appear underfoot, circular and celestial, rippling and shimmering with a sense of the cosmic. The four prick up their ears, casting their eyes towards a ridgeline in the middle distance, several metres high perhaps, where meltwater spills out in cascades, steadily flooding the marshy coast on which they stand.

Against the wishes of the others, Wally chronicles and finds the runoff to be of astonishing scale, raging down from the mountains, from the heart of Antarctica. They each knew it, but overlaying the surface reality there and then with data visualisation closes a psychological gap, a distance through which a stealthy denial of the horror could be maintained, many hopelessly hopeful dreams flourishing, until whatever final moment awaits them all.

Wally flicks it to their lenses. They reluctantly accept the information.

In the time it takes John to make a few curses in a suitably ancient tongue, a shared sense of anguish—but also, oddly, of awe—at the scale of loss silences them, bringing them to a standstill and, in Evie's case, her knees.

There is silence, stunning and simple. And bereavement. A harmonic *How?* How had this come to be, the impossible pace of the greatest changes in human history, running away beyond solving, out of reach? Out of time.

Ice, the last holdout of an ancient geology, of an Earth uninterrupted, has now been indelibly altered. That permafrost brace, a constant against the climbing scale of cataclysms—disease, hunger, war, catastrophe—is melting by the gigatonne. That once-solid symbol liquifies at a rate which can only go in one direction, rippling out across time, capping off the world.

They swivel around, their feet locked to the disappearing place beneath, and share in its loss. Muted, they huddle together as flightless winged creatures once did here. After years of cataloguing the decline, their bodies hum in tired agreement that hope can no longer hold them, tipped as far as we are. The time has come to retreat to their various homelands to wait out another pulse, another rise, another fall.

IN THE BACKWASH of Ushuaia's toughened shoreline, Wally and John skip stones, rippling the grey cloudland apart. The dark, concentric rings of each plop, moving ever further apart, still them. Having waved Arne and Evie off to Santiago, bound west across the Pacific, they stand close now, sharing warmth and the silent feeling departure brings. They mumble here and there, admiring one another's legerdemain as they skip their way along the beach, redefined across these rising years, but rough and undisturbed as before.

Until now.

The accelerating melt across the planet, the sense of an ending, draws eager witnesses into the Beagle Channel. They leave footprints here on Argentina's very own end of the world—the beginning of everything. Wally recalls the sparkling, variegated city of decades before, documented for his own purposes—and perhaps, in hindsight, for his own gain. The year-round mildness has given way to extremes both freezing and scorching. Signs of enterprise now slip across the fueguine architecture of colourful *casitas* and gabled roofs, the port serving fear and fascination alike, funnelling wealth upwards into havens safe from the vagaries of a collapsing biosphere.

John gives the dawdling Wally a nudge and nods north towards the Martial Mountains, the late morning sun revealing their black snowlessness. Each knows what the other thinks. They keep moving, passing a trio of fisherwomen preparing to head out, before arriving at a boat ramp, from which they make their way up to the esplanade. Pausing for breath, they gaze out in the direction of the great melt they witnessed just days ago, a seismic event, condensed for billions down to soundbites and snippets and updates.

John grunts and Wally understands.

After a silence both would rather not end, Wally asks, 'What will you do now?'

John winces, mulling it over. Seagulls squawk around the harbour, indifferent to history. He barks above them, 'Fuck knows. No place to go, anyway.'

Staring at his fading companion, Wally cannot help but share the feeling. They were finally cast adrift, irreversibly loosened from the delicate planetary conditions that made up life. Gliding out of the goldilocks zone. To contemplate it was to stare into an unnavigable abyss, and therein, Wally thought, lay the problem all along. The human problem.

And only John, of all the brilliant people Wally has known in his prolonged life, can cut to the heart of such horror.

'Never mind, Wal,' he says. 'The view will be better without us, believe me.'

Wally forces a chuckle, then is overcome by anxious laughter and affection. They embrace, Wally holding John up a little.

'Hungry?' Wally asks, easing John back down.

'I'm ravenous.'

'I know a place nearby.'

Vehicles, deadly silent and sound, slide by in both directions. You can't trust your ears for distance here, save for the spray of wheels on the wet road. Old vehicles here and there, running on old reserves, striking yet dreadful relics over which Wally and John both glower and ogle. The moment they step out to cross the road, the vehicles come to a uniform stop, except those odd few pumping out greenhouse gases, halting a human second later.

The wind picks up, tunnelling down the street as Wally and John tighten their coats. Wally takes John's hand and guides him down a side street and into a small café buzzing with family and togetherness. Gazing at the humble storefront—the simple glasswork and aluminium edging, the frayed, printed menus and advertisements—John feels as if he has ventured back in time fifty years, maybe more. Stepping through, tapping along the crumbling linoleum, Wally nods brief thanks to the youth—a teenage son or nephew within the family business, John presumes—who is waiting the four or five tables in the confined space and they tuck into a corner table.

They order a deranged array of local delights: sizzling asado with chimichurri, followed by churros with yerba maté, the straws of which they share back and forth in that unselfconscious, intimate manner they've fallen into over the years.

Wally wipes at the window with his sleeve, clearing their view.

'I won't be going back home,' John suddenly declares.

Wally gazes over him, quietly curious.

'Australia is fucked. I've done all I can. Maybe it's selfish—I dunno—but I don't have many years left.'

Wally tightens inside, a guilt he cannot untie.

John catches him and holds his hands up in the air. 'You need to stop with that fucking shit. Moping about your bio-privilege. I still intend to outlive you, naturally. That's what's keeping me here, dickhead!'

Hysterical, John attempts to order *dos cervezas*, confusing the poor young waiter until Wally clarifies that, yes, they do want beers, even after all the dessert they've just downed. Who knows when they will see each other again?

'So,' Wally begins, 'are you going roaming again, old scholar?'

'Something like that,' John indicates, pondering the impossible. 'If it's really all in freefall, don't you want to be out there to see it? And I don't mean the colonising shit you do—and, by the way, I believe you still owe me for some of that work—but just witnessing the world, documenting it. What other choice is there?'

Wally nods, ambivalent but conceding. 'No fight left?'

'Fuck off, Wal. I'll never stop fighting. But people'—John waves out violently at the foggy world—'gave up on ideas a long time ago.'

Ideas could have saved them, once, in a more privileged age. Now confusion—hurt—abounds. Wally sees it wherever he goes, chronicling the collapse, that disbelief at something—some simple carbon combustion, progress—which ignited many years before anyone alive today was born.

'Do you think we've thought of everything?' Wally asks.

'Of course not.'

'What do you make of Arne's rewilding plans?'

John waves it away. 'Sounds like whitefella stuff to me. Fairly certain it will drive Evie nuts, y'know. Eat carrots for a bit longer while everywhere else burns!'

Wally falls silent.

John picks up a charred corner of flesh left untouched from their main course and scrutinises his dear old friend. He points with a flailing bone, ribbing him: 'But you're up to something, aren't you? You've got that clever fucking look about you.'

'No,' Wally declares flatly.

'Bullshit. I know that look on your smart face. You're squirming, mate.'

'I'm dead still.'

'Yeah, you tell yourself that. But you've got some scheme going on, don't you?'

Outside, Wally spots solarised lorries gliding by on the high street, transporting materials to this end-times frontier. In a year or so, the place will be booming. Until the final ice shelves carve apart and flood this land of fire. Across the world, coastlines are being radically reshaped. Extreme sea-level rise was locked in by the 2030s, the oceans thermally expanding with each fraction of a degree. Since then, they have all simply been waiting.

Wally is tired of it. Of his life. Of waiting. Of having done very little, despite the adulation he's received. And in that moment, Wally confesses to John that it is he who has no fight left. That he is out of ideas and, in desperation, has begun to think in unthinkable ways.

John tilts his head, frowning ever so gently. Wally catches the profound concern, genuine and so rare in his life now. It cracks him open, and he spills forth death and desperation.

'We are running out of options,' Wally explains. 'These are extreme times.'

'What the fuck are you playing at?'

'I've been working with Freddie. Sort of. And Kim.'

John does not hesitate to move, paying up and pushing his companion out into the street. 'C'mon, buddy. Let's go for a walk.' Lost for direction, John pulls Wally along, who, though briefly wanting to suggest they ought to head in the other direction, towards the port, accepts the decisively aimless tow. The late-afternoon wind bites at them now.

Marching along, looking straight ahead, John demands, 'How did you find him?'

'I never really lost him,' Wally admits.

'You know he's a terrorist, right? And Kim too?'

Wally stops in his tracks, reaching to turn John around. He shrugs, *I guess so*, resisting the urge to correct John concerning Kim. They both stand still, taking in the harbour, catching their breath, visibly pluming between them in the temperature drop. 'Listen, I haven't done anything yet,' Wally says.

'So, what, they want you to help them out? Fund them?'

Wally shakes his head. 'No. They seem to have plenty of that. Freddie wants information.'

'*The Chronicle?*'

Wally nods, ready for a scolding. Minutes pass between them, frozen as forever.

Eventually, John asks, 'Have you decided what you're going to do?'

Wally shakes his head, his tall frame shivering a little.

John looks out, winding back through the years to younger, more hopeful versions of themselves. The further back he went, the more stable things were—or at least seem from here. He's not ready to let that version of Wally—that version of themselves, Freddie and Kim included—go just yet.

'It seems to me, Wal, that we've got no place to be, right?'

Wally looks up, catching that infectious mischief he first fell for decades ago. 'What chaos have you got planned?'

'I'm thinking you and me. We go on a bit more. Go north and check out this continent while we still can. Plenty of time for seeing. Plenty of time for talking, figuring shit out. You can fly back to Canada whenever you like, and I'll just go my own way. What d'ya reckon?'

In a flash, Wally feels the relief that only old company can bring, bound as they are by shared time and loss. The terminus of the moment is clear—as are the various directions he could move along at this juncture—and Wally knows instinctively where to go.

'Sounds good, John.'

15

SEASTEAD

Carbon dioxide parts per million: 639.4

Deep within the Pacific zone of the United Nations of Seasteads, where millions of the dislanded struggle to stay afloat, Freddie lets his mind slip across the percolating sea, homing in, riding up through the great towers in the far distance, visualising the intricate pieces of one final, explosive hurrah.

This seahood—Stanley—serves the worst *notsky* in the district. Freddie relishes the ersatz whisky, basking in the lowliness.

'You're not Jesus,' Kim interrupts, handing him another shot of horror. 'You—we—are free to leave whenever.'

Taking it, he inclines his head. 'I cannot. I will not.'

She scoffs. 'Honour keeping you here?'

'Something like that.' He is unsettlingly calm, more so than usual. Something about his demeanour troubles Kim—something new, something bright, something dangerous. She gives him a look: *What have you done now?*

Leaning back on his upturned fire drum, he raises his hands in innocence. 'Nothing...yet.'

'But...'

Freddie looks around the dank and fetid tavern, a caverned space like every other carved out illegally beneath the platforms, squaloring below the waterline, swarming with ears. He raises a large, oily hand, black with work. 'Not now. Where is Raph?'

'Out on assignment. Delivery.'

Freddie withdraws a logbar from one of the many pockets of his boilersuit, splitting it to share with Kim. She gets started on it right away. It's stale but still sweet, cracking loudly, resounding through her skull. Freddie continues. 'He seems to enjoy it—exploitation.'

'Careful, *Marx*. He's one of us, you know,' Kim says.

Freddie's colourless, blue eyes slice through the din, flaring with brutal doubt, a zealous certainty.

'He's your nephew, Freddie!'

'A nephew who aspires too much,' he sneers, yelling through a whisper. 'I've tried. But some things cannot be changed. It was a mistake to bring him in.'

Kim softens, thinking of the man they saved and the delayed sense of motherhood she came to feel through him, a dormant desire. A silent longing to rewrite the past has grown in her of late. Evenings, she plays it out in her quarters, plugging into parturition sims, augmenting reality. But it's never enough; instead of raising beautiful little beings, she has spent her life making beautiful things—tech used for questionable means towards uncertain ends.

Kim fires up. 'What will you do then? Turn him over to Gaia?' She downs her shot and slams it on the small metal bench separating them.

Freddie appears indifferent, his expression unchanged, startlingly beautiful.

She cannot bear the silence he enforces. 'Well?'

Freddie sighs languidly, shifting his proud body her way. 'Kimmy, you know that's not up to me. That will depend on what Raph does. He is the master of his own fate.'

Emptiness drifts between them, a great chasm only Kim can see. On the edge of breaking, Kim looks up at Freddie and promises, 'Raph is fine. He'll be fine.'

'He enjoys running the deliveries—the labour of the Steads—to the towers too much.'

'He's scouting, Freddie.'

'He's dreaming, again. Aspiring. I worry he has not changed—not really. He would gladly rise up the towers and take a place among the exalted. I'm sure of it.' Freddie slams the table abruptly. 'The ones who destroyed this planet!' he yells. 'The ones who took everything!'

Around him, the drunk and deworlded take tired umbrage, recognising a comrade, vaguely echoing Freddie's chant, before returning each to their own internal miseries.

'Wouldn't you?' Kim says, near to trembling.

'No,' he declares, resolute and absolute. 'You know I could get us in there, Kimmy. The longevity treatments too. I am not tempted, even in these times. The same end will come to us all.'

Kim isn't so sure.

LATER, AS THE SUN ARCS DOWN towards the horizon, flicking cinders of burnt light across the water, glimmering like hope all around the seastead communities, the many thousands of floating, multi-acre hexagonal platforms—grotesque new ground linked together for miles, far and wide, a vast swathe of history's failures great enough to make a nation—burn orange in the day's fade.

Kim takes the rickety bridge out of Stanley, escaping through the marginally less hungry districts of Elwood, Waterside and Tower's Ride, outer seasteads which, situated by the water, provide points of supply to the towers. The labour comes from the centre, deep within the nameless and numbered factory platforms, of which even Freddie keeps clear.

Wrapping her rags around her, concealed in the zonal fashion, she walks quietly along the weather-torn jetty, taking in the distance, where the tips of several heaven-high towers needle out of the horizon, piercing through the haze from a day away. At the goods and services waypoint, Kim presents her forged and tragically backstoried documents.

Free to go, she skips ahead to Docking Bay 94, where Raph is running maintenance on a skimmer. She creeps up on him, moving silently along the gangway. 'Boo!'

Raph doesn't flinch, focused as he is on repairing a component of the watercraft. After a few seconds he gets up, turning. He smiles, delighted as ever to see Kim.

'How was your day, Kay?' he asks.

He's the only person who ever asks her this; she assumes she is the only one who ever asks him, too.

'Not bad,' Kim says. 'Did some countings out past the Crait district. Deaths are going down. People are coalescing, rationing as a herd.'

'That's good,' says Raph, cleaning his hands, still smiling sweetly. 'That's a start.'

A reformed man, he's grown handsome these years, balding a little but swelling with purpose, pride. He is everything compared to his former, snivelling self. His belief is infectious. It buoys Kim today, when she needs it the most. The sun sinks behind his shoulder.

She asks him about his day, at which he simply shrugs. 'All the same. Transports.'

He moves across the skimmer towards her, the vessel pitching a little as he comes around, stooping beside her, wrapping an arm around her thinning frame. They absorb the vista, motionless but for the serene, out-of-this-world bob.

Frigatebirds swoop through, ranging out across the near distance, along Raph's diurnal delivery course.

'I left bits for them,' Raph says, playful and leaning into Kim. 'You wouldn't believe what *they*'—he juts his chin towards the towers—'throw away.'

'You've forgotten who you're talking to, kid.' In a flash Kim remembers all the inner-city dumpsters of the world she had crawled through back in the twenties and thirties, redistributing food to the streets. A quaint, grassroots time, fastened to a larger sense of rebellion. Such things felt like hope at the time, until Freddie, consuming every single update of Wally's blasted chronicle, grew tired of inaction.

'Sorry. I meant that in a kind way,' Kim clarifies.

Darkness falls around them. The derelict lights lining the wharf begin flickering on and off.

'I know,' Raph replies, but Kim is veering elsewhere, slowing her mind, focusing. They sit in silence, the moment stretching on.

They have hidden here for so long now that Kim knows the performative movements of every hour. And, in a place paraded across the remaining world as one of the great humanitarian projects, built in truth to serve the longevous and wealthy, individual digressions from this daily loop are rare. She senses a disturbance.

Raph is unaware of any shifts, subtle or otherwise, in the steady rhythms. From his pack he removes some parcels of food for them, accompanied by surplus—contraband—water capsules.

Kim tightens, the adumbrations of some horror moving through her. She trembles.

Noticing this, Raph takes her hand. 'What's wrong? You okay? You're freaking me out.'

'Something's wrong.' She scans back along the wharf. The so-called market square of Tower's Ride a few hundred metres away is conspicuously empty. She senses Raph's unease catching up to hers. The air around them settles down to nothing, as though sucked into the great cosmic vacuum glittering above, casting their lives into insignificance.

'What is it?' Raph begs, the lines of his brow furrowing in the moonlight.

'Freddie,' she manages, hissing.

'What about him?'

'Something isn't right.'

'Nothing's ever right with Freddie, Kim.'

'No—I mean, look around. The steads. They're dead tonight.'

'Maybe just around here. So what?'

Kim patches into various cams, flicking through views of quietened alleyways that should, at this hour, be bustling with all manner of mayhem and debauchery. Instead, only a few souls linger in each frame, perplexed by the spectral emptiness. She flicks the view to Raph's lenses to see what he makes of it.

Disturbed, he guesses, 'A ceasework?'

Kim neighs. 'Yeah, right. What are the chances? Besides, if the steads had been issued a ceasework because of infection or supply issues, we'd know. It goes out steadwide generally, and lockdown is invoked. Last one happened just before we infiltrated here.'

Raph nods, taking in her sound reasoning.

Kim receives a notification from Freddie. It's written in turgid, circular terms—some old code the two of them used decades ago for secret operations and loving epistolary alike. Beyond its meaning, it moves her—until she deciphers it.

Raph sees her eyes widen, a shock rippling through her features. She looks up at him jaggedly, struggling to breathe. 'Your last run. What was it?'

'I don't know—it's always cased up. The same as usual, I guess. I'm scouting, remember, not smuggling.'

'We need to get out of here.'

'What the fuck? What's going on?'

'Raph, now! Let's go.'

She grabs him by the arm, and they run across the gangway, building to a sprint along the wharf. Raph struggles to keep up with her astonishing pace, the movements of someone who has survived the game this long.

Then a distant series of low concussions brings them to a standstill, rattling through their skulls, ringing in their ears.

Kim's shoulders slump for a moment, before she darts sideways to skip through the sheds towards the other side of the wharf, trying to understand what is happening. Winding around, Raph follows her, moving through the skimmer yards, out of which he stumbles and lands on her heels, nearly bowling them both into the slosh.

He takes his place beside her, the hammering still ringing out across the dark, quaking through the Earth and the ocean, tingling the soles of their tired feet. Together in terror, in step with one another, they move out slowly along a disused jetty—a walking plank, now.

Out of that horrifying sound, drumming like war, comes a blinding light that sears the horizon. They turn away instinctively. Shielding their eyes, they look back to see the towers, one after the other, firing like distant torches, semaphoring the end of the world as they know it.

16

EDEN

Carbon dioxide parts per million: 628.2

Out here, wandering the end of the Earth, she passes silently through the ribbons of scorched land that are said to lead her home. Daylight burns above, radiating through the wings of a creature whose name she has forgotten, circling the sun in a way that throws Jasmine back to days of play—the textured dreams of her father's embrace, her mother's songful whisper.

Off the trail, through the blackened columns, her heart—the child—makes mischief, toddling in and out of the empty places that seem so full to her, so delightful. She plays as if this place ought never change. They have travelled far; the girl has seen too much in only a few years of living. Whatever playgrounds she makes of broken places, who is Jasmine to rob her of such brief wonder? She keeps her distance, knowing the resilience Aloy will need in this world and the next.

Under the weight of their gear, Jasmine focuses on the hard path ahead, ears twigging all the while, tracking the movements of that precious little being, who is climbing and tumbling through the flanking wasteland.

Further on, they come together just as Aloy is running out of breath, at a fork where an ancient and overgrown path leads inland, and another, freshly cleared by trampling, leads to the coast. Jasmine leans to the latter, seeking salt on the air that isn't there. Worry, plain and sickening, strikes. A motherly fear she buries every morning surfaces.

Aloy sees it; Jasmine sees that she sees it, and they each lie through silence, protecting one another as they have done since the beginning of life, which for Jasmine might as well have begun with Aloy. All the years before that Earth-splitting moment pale, disintegrate into the unknowability of a stranger's life.

The child, born in a year of great reckoning, knows little of the past but for passer-by snippets: people lining along dustbowl roads or strangers nestled in the vast array of fading cities—abandoned boroughs, vanishing townships, gated metropolises holding on to the old ways of *growth*—describing equally the time of her birth as some long-ago cataclysm, pondering omens, trying to reverse history.

But she is a budding reconstructionist, assembling dioramas out of the pastel-blue leaves that have returned this season at last, sprouting from the deathbed of forests—a growth so true it prickles with cruel hope.

Along their journey, the child has re-enacted each late history, closing in on the truth.

Later that night, camped by lamplight at the side of the path by the fork, Aloy is on the mark, her thesis near completion. Oblivious to the oppressive air, she narrates her play leafily, something Jasmine remembers her own mother doing a long time ago, tucking her into a soft and safe bed.

A great unseen thing is happening now, in the backdrop. As the beautiful little blue leaf people go about their impossibly happy lives, a thing they've done but cannot see keeps growing behind them, around them, beneath them, above them. Aloy flicks dirt about and makes propelling, furious engine-like sounds, forcing air through her teeth. The leaves, caught by surprise, become ever more trapped, unable to escape. The animal leaves—a tiger, a dolphin and a bird—sink with them too. In a final act, Aloy pulls two frail leaves from behind and marches them along the remnants of her play, concluding, 'But Aloy and Mum keep going.'

Jasmine falters. She looks out across the undulating terrain, visibly mudcracked and contracted even in the fading light, broken in so many ways. This soundless world echoes nothing, bears no resemblance to the places she once knew.

Lost, she shuffles towards her daughter and lifts her into her lap, dispensing the final portion of her own meagre meal down a generation. Aloy takes the sacrificed morsel involuntarily. Her hunger, like her spirit, has no limit.

Unable to speak, Jasmine simply strokes the child's silken hair behind her ears, over and over. She wants to sing but in the moment wavers, wondering where song could come from. One by one the stars come out to play, the unchanged celestial realm boasting its permanence, its grand structure. Question time begins.

'Mum?'

'Yes, my heart,' Jasmine replies, resting her chin against the top of her daughter's head. Aloy had only recently—and far too soon—stopped calling her *Mummy*.

That voice, far too mature in rhythm and measure, entreats, 'Where are we going?'

'You know where, baby.' Jasmine enfolds the bone-hungry child ever tighter in her wiry arms, waiting out time.

'But I want to hear you say it.' She tilts her head back and looks up over her little shoulders at her mother. 'Tell me more about it.'

When she tries to speak of it, Jasmine struggles to give the dream any voice, any life. 'It's somewhere...'

'Somewhere green?'

'Somewhere green,' Jasmine confirms, nodding.

'How far is it?'

'Not far.'

'What will it be like when we get there?'

'Well, it will be wonderful.'

'Promise?'

'I promise.'

'Will there be other kids?'

'Yes, I imagine so.'

A stillness settles in. Aloy drifts sleepwards, mumbling questions all the way down, breathing deep between each word.

'Is. It. Real?'

'Is what real, baby?' Jasmine intones, smelling and stroking the child's sweet crown with the last of her day's strength.

'The. Place.'

And before Jasmine has to answer, Aloy is off, descending into a restful place of which Jasmine can only daydream. Groaning, she raises the child, carrying the full weight of her over to their tent. As she tucks the child in, Aloy appears smaller, frail, nuzzled beneath thinning muslin.

Outside, Jasmine sits still for a long while, sipping tea and turning to thoughts she will only entertain alone, on watch. Beginnings and endings rise and fall across the stars. *What could have been* and *what will be* branch off in her mind; she manages to settle into the now, into the present tense of her twilight. *Aloy and Mum keep going.* Even now, deteriorating as she is, the strength this childly maxim gives her is beyond counting.

She wants to sleep but knows it isn't safe yet. Will it ever be?

In the far distance below, lights like fairies scatter through the basin. A convoy of people. Likely harmless, she calculates, running against everything stories had for centuries told people about their nature. She wants to reach out across the vast distance and hold them, gather the golden specks in her palms and whisper wishful things.

The surrounding deadwood creaks and splinters and she jumps, mistaking it briefly for life before returning to her one true task. She sets about securing the camp, cleaning and packing their gear—portable solars, obsoleting devices, utensils, provisions, threads—before turning inward to listen to her heart, the brave child sleeping deep and peaceful nearby.

As Jasmine takes stock of all they have, a visceral panic rushes through her; time is setting on them.

Before retiring, she pores over her cloaked binary beacon, the bracelet she wears to communicate with the dead, the complex, coded sequence of messages her oracle uncle left to guide her home to safety. She mutters on and off, 'Wal, what are we doing here? Where do we go?'

She waits forever. The moon bursts out from behind the inland mountain range, arcing high and illumining the jutting expanse of the island they traversed over the past few days. Nothing comes to her from the beyond; the device is dying, its light flickering out. Maps and devices won't find this place, this myth.

She wants to scream but lacks the force. They should have stayed put and fought through hunger, disaster and disease. A world away, now. But she breathes and focuses on the promised place, the story she has told Aloy over and over in the witching hours, day after day.

Hauling the last of their gear off the main path, Jasmine methodically lines up what little they have in the vestibule of their tent before turning in and collapsing beside her daughter.

In the morning, Aloy and Jasmine will keep going.

17

THE GREAT
REWILDING

Carbon dioxide parts per million: 628.2

In the afterburn of the world there is a great rewilding. Deviants scatter out over the planet into dusty cells, ploughing on towards the great green dream. Loosely connected, the communities exchange knowledge over distances once small, either through the old unreliable information highways that still hum up above or by utterance, passing seeds from hand to hand, land to land. They are bound by the most revolutionary and yet simplest idea in the world: *regrowth*.

Passive, they watch the nascent growth from a distance. It is not a human idea, after all, its provenance written eternally in wood, reaching back into the deep past of plantae, to a place most could not even imagine, let alone understand. But, more and more, they come to recognise their place among such growing grace, slowing life down, quietening. And, after much observation and debate, the message relayed widely is that the best thing they can do is practically nothing, for an age.

Wondrous ancient technologies rise up together, outstretching the collective global endeavour of humanity in a matter of years. A singular design that cleanses the air, captures carbon, conserves water and preserves soil, beckoning sundry other life to join in its patient yet immense movement, and, from a human point of view, instils calm where there would be none in the long fade-out.

But amid the fray of halted cities, their bunkered and crater-scored fringes, and the encroaching desert of the world, these sanctuaries come merely to freckle the Earth green. And, as throughout history, people home in on edens.

KNEELING DOWN, placing a palm to the soft, needled floor of the understorey, Arne tries to raise that old hearing, the fanciful and deep-rooted affinity he felt for trees. His knees creak and ache, waiting for a miracle. But nothing comes. If he's honest—pragmatic—he knows it never did; knowledge once gave him the sense of it, filled him with such young awe. But that answer is too grim to entertain this afternoon: *Let's play pretend awhile.* He recalls loosely some of the processes by which they signal out to one another. Complex networks of meaning, singing through the air and trading underground. It comes as mild relief that the signification of their kind was never fully decoded, a little mystery buzzing on forever in the chaos.

He looks around, mouth agape, astounded even after all these years here watching life on autopilot. The sense of estrangement is, as ever, real, storylike, as if some deceased relation has returned from the earth. This might be a forest yet.

A group of co-wilders—youthful beyond Arne's comfort—pass him abruptly, joking in their stride as they move through the juvenile grove of gums and pencil pines.

He moves to catch them up on the rise, attempting to best his years. At the peak, he looks out over the modular community—their home—stationed one hundred and fifty to two hundred years in from the shoreline, the rows of rotatable bamboo abodes and communal structures fenestrated with transparent photovoltaics and affixed with custom tankages, swivelling ventage, all nestled within an emergent greenery, a canopy to be.

Arne tries to conceal his panting and sweating beneath the sheer degree of late-century heat. In his blurring periphery he senses the group of twenty-somethings nudging elbows, nodding towards him and sniggering. They hush the jeers as best they know how. He resists the horrible urge to lecture them, to demand respect. He knows the quiet hierarchy here and abides by community conventions of andragogy.

Instead, he looks past the divide, commenting on the view, gesturing out in that shrunken way people of his years now do, bodily apologetic. They find common ground here and, to Arne's surprise, as the group set about trekking off ahead at their natural pace, they bid him farewell, calling him by name. He fails to reply and simply raises an embarrassed hand as they pass.

Once they are out of sight, he slumps down and takes his rest on a log bench made for contemplation. His gaze drifts beyond the land, searching the mysterious body out there, still beautiful to this day; he cannot pick out Evie and her school of skimmers. They could be off the horizon by this hour, gliding back just before nightfall, as is their wont.

His device warbles—a custom tone, an extinct variety of butcherbird. Virgil wants to see him. Rising to his feet, he sets off for Central.

Yet here he is now, amid the rebuild, a key figure in the formation of something new.

'Walk with me, Arne,' he insists, brow furrowing beneath the peak of his old, sweat-lined baseball cap, homage to a forgotten passion with which he fidgets to no end.

Arne follows his march.

'Report's come in of someone at the Embrace,' he explains.

Arne hurries along. 'Any other info?'

Virgil indicates not, before striding off in the direction of the road that rises steadily up into the tableland and hopping into a cart. 'Get in, Arnie.'

'Thank Christ!' Arne hollers, catching up. 'Thought you were going to make us do one of your Earth-forsaken hikes.'

Virgil twirls balletically around in his seat. He scoffs, smiling that genial Concord smile. 'You millennials got no legs.'

'That's because some of us are getting old.'

Virgil nods, approving. 'And that's admirable of you. The same fate as everyone here. You're just a little further along the path than most, is all. *Time is a flat circle*, or whatever it is. But we're walking once we get up top. I insist.'

'I've been out all day, completing my quota!'

'You always go over anyway. What's a little more?'

Arne throws his hands up, exhausted. 'It's a few too many miles! Please, Virg. I'm tired.'

The comrade's shoulders soften, hands loosening on the wheel. 'Tell you what—let's ride up the climb and we'll take the final flat on foot. Silently.'

Relieved, Arne agrees.

On the ride up, the lightweight engine whirring quietly throughout, Virgil rattles on, circling a subject for as long as he can.

'You know I'll be fifty next year?' he says. Arne didn't, but could have guessed. 'My time will be up soon. Someone younger will need to take my place. The way of things here.'

'Will you stay on?' Arne asks.

Virgil scowls, mulling it over. He takes a corner sharply, then selects a lower gear as they start their sharp ascent. 'I'm inclined to think not.'

Arne nods, a lengthy but chummy silence overcoming them.

Further along, Virgil quips, 'We could leave together. Back to the city life. You and Evie. Not too late to climb aboard the longevity train, Arnie, my man!'

Arne sees how Virgil's brisk laughter is replaced in a flash by a grave longing, his heart, like Arne's, lost somewhere in yesteryears, empires and old glories.

Miles later, Arne begins to speculate. 'I was thinking of nominating.'

Virgil stares sidelong at him, taken aback. 'Nominating? No one's done that in years. There's no viable land left!'

'Oh, I have some spots in mind. Done the research.'

'I'm sure you have. But trying to get that through the council'
—he takes his hands off the wheel for a split second, raising them
dramatically—'best of luck to you.'

As they flatten out, spying in the far distance the Embrace, an
immense, overly dramatic gateway fashioned from the weatherworn
carcasses of perished trees, they disembark.

They strike out. Arne tries to summon the energy to keep up
the pace, but only a few steps in he finds he cannot.

Virgil turns back to see his friend gazing long at the gate, as
if possessed. Looking back towards the Embrace, Virgil raises
his binoculars and makes out a figure carrying something in its
arms. 'A visitor.'

Arne senses something else flickering at the edge of Virgil's
greying countenance. 'Marauders?'

'No, not marauders, Arne.' Virgil begins to chuckle, having
seen so much worse. 'Just a visitor. All alone.'

'Well, let's do what we always do. Let them in, put them up
for a few days.'

They nod, uneasy. The community is only just holding on,
already at capacity. The drought of the recent monoseason has
reduced their catch and yield by a third this year. Those opting
for parenthood, whether they be couples, thruples or larger partnerships, will have to put their dreams on hold. The thought
saddens Arne.

He quickly takes up the binoculars, yanking them from Virgil.
Peering through, sweating, he struggles to bring the figure into
focus, its silhouette miragelike and dancing on the heat.

A stabbing sensation courses through Arne. *Could it be?* Perhaps
it's just some old acquaintances passing through. But some other
vision—a dream he's dreamed a thousand times, and for Evie
perhaps even more—sparks him to life, pushing him forward at
a manic pace. A panic—a need to know—courses through him,
surging from deep within parts of himself he has not tapped into
in years.

Directly ahead, the sun is coming down low and orange, flaring the view. Apparitions drift on the road. To its side, the endless scraggle of bushland whiffs of burning and trauma. For the final few hundred metres he shields his eyes.

At the Embrace, he finds a dark silhouette melting in the sun, floating. The bedraggled figure lurches forward, stumbling out of the glare and into striking view, peering through the gaps in the gate, the cracks in Arne.

His breath leaves him, as it did at her birth. He loses his feet, his speech. A vision, a second coming: his daughter, stoic through wild hunger, carrying something—someone—in her wiry arms.

'Jazzy,' he gasps.

'Hello, Dad,' says his angel, stumbling and on the edge of oblivion. 'You going to let me in?'

18

THIRD ROCK FROM THE FIRE

Carbon dioxide parts per million: 603.37

Nightfall; a strange time.

Around the campfire, a man and a girl draw circles in the dirt with sticks loosed from the branches of windfallen gums. Legions of tormented wood angels, thrown down, strewn across the great valley they'd wandered that day, heading for the coastline. Intimate and whorled lives upturned, their split innards showing their age in broken rings—broken seasons. The man—Arne—accounted for some of the fallen giants, all far older and, in his estimation, far nobler than himself.

He is starting to forget their names—those which colonising humans, in their impossible task of collecting everything, gave them centuries before. *Eucalyptus viminalis. Eucalyptus nitens. Eucalyptus sieberi.* They have truer names, of course. The man has come, in time, to know that—he feels its truth in the parts he holds now as he traces shapes in the earth with his only granddaughter, Aloy.

He looks to her, beside him. She is swirling her branchlet, arm extended and making clear, decisive marks in the ground. A picture is forming. Of what exactly he cannot tell. As always, she does her own thing. Always will. He is merely partaking, dabbling. He tries not to cross her looping lines.

As she focuses on her masterplan, her voice rises like a distant fog. 'What was this place, Granddad?'

He considers this for a while, his furrowed brow clear by fire's light. 'A national park.'

'What's that?'

'A place.'

'What kind of place?'

This one's even harder. He looks to the stars for consolation and constellation. 'People used to come here. In great droves. In search of nature, or what they thought was nature...or something like that.'

'I see. But isn't that what we're doing now?'

'I guess so.'

She moves around the fire and, returning her stick to the earth, expands her oeuvre out into a wider space. She pulls her thickly woven cowl tight to her neck and begins, once again, to ask questions of her grandfather, all the while concentrating on her work. How many she has asked in her life he cannot say. Thousands and more. Right from when she was very little, preparing for the world to come.

'Was it always so cold here?'

He almost laughs. 'You think this is cold?'

She looks directly at him for the first time tonight and nods. Her green eyes are devastating. He rarely gets to see them. Children look away from their elders now. *Planet eaters*, they each and all think. They are not wrong. The man sees this for the very inevitable thing that it is: take their world away—their air, their food, their safety—and they will turn away from you.

Her eyes, like the forgotten green of the oldest and most dense of rainforests, give him permission to continue.

'Used to be colder,' he explains, bracing his arms around his old, stiff body. 'Much colder, in fact. Winters here on the promontory, by the water.' He looks down towards the cove, dark and still but for flakes of moonglow shimmering on the seawater. He tries to remember the old shoreline. Where it began and where it ended in the shifting tide, before the first pulse. They are safe from high tide here, a metre above sea level—its rise humanly slow, geologically rapid. You could settle here for a night, but not a life.

Arne looks back over his shoulder to the headland, the break he used to surf. He can just make out its shape in the night, pretend nothing had ever changed, filling the land with the details of old, wondrous memories. He would like her to see it as he does—as he did. He wishes the world had a better plan for her.

An intent little statue, she waits. She is not satisfied and wants more. He sighs before continuing. 'Cold fronts would come in all the way from Antarctica. Not the kinds of storms we have now. But icy winds that battered the coast here. Rain like bullets. Beautiful, now that I think about it. Though back then we used to hide from that sort of thing, duck back into a tent or something. The weather felt extreme.'

'Antarctica? The ice place?'

He nods.

Content, the girl continues to make mysterious wrinkles in the dirt.

Whirling, the man focuses now on the gift he has for his grand-daughter, stowed deep in the bottom of his pack, which sits behind them by a charred stump of wood at the edge of the fire. A feeling like regret flickers through him. He suspects he's made an error but knows he cannot take it back. The gift must be dealt with.

'Come over here,' he says, inching nervously towards his pack. For just the second time tonight she looks up, wary beneath her hood, meeting his gaze. She circles slowly, stick in hand, around the dexter side of the fire to join him.

'I have something for you,' he says, trying to sound excited as he begins to rummage through his pack.

'What is it?'

He reaches right in and pulls out a fist-sized parcel wrapped in cloth, blotched with brown stains and damp with melted ice.

He offers it to her, inviting her to take it from his hands. She does so, drawing the parcel to her chest.

She gags immediately, dropping it to the ground. 'What is that?'

'Meat. For us.'

She does not hesitate. She raises her stick to his throat. 'Why would you bring that with you? You know what can follow us!'

He's ashamed. 'I know.'

'Is it real?'

'Yes. *Real* real.'

'What do you mean?'

'It's real meat. Not the fake stuff. This type of meat, it's hard to get. Have to trade for it. We should eat it quick.'

'No, *you* should. It needs to disappear.'

Arne kneels down to collect the fallen flesh. She gags again, though less viscerally this time. To his surprise, his granddaughter begins to laugh. 'That smells gross. I can't believe how much of this stuff you all used to eat.'

Her chirp is like no other sound in all his memory, a salve like honey that might keep him here on the Earth a little longer.

'Me neither,' he agrees. 'But I wanted to share it with you. And then you can share with me what you've drawn.' He looks her over, remembering how fat kids and teenagers used to be. He slowly encircles a free hand around her upper arm. 'You are all so skinny these days.'

She pulls away. 'I'm fine.'

'I know you are.' He unwraps the cloth, the dank musk of meat wafting between them. 'If you don't want any, I understand. But I don't know if I can eat all this by myself.'

'You'll have to.'

He raises his eyebrows, looks down to consider the strange lump in his palms. 'I don't know.'

She moves closer to him and slips both her arms around one of his. She leans against his shoulder, looking at the gift. 'Eat what you can, and if you can't finish it...'

'What?'

'Let's just see. But we need to get rid of it.'

'I know. I just want it gone,' he says, remorseful.

'You're an old fool.'

'True.'

Later, as the meat bursts and hisses, hanging over the fire from what was his drawing stick—an article imbued with great powers of creation—the old man wonders if he can remember how to cook the stuff. But even after all these years it comes to him.

Satisfied at the browning, he brings it down into his lap and slices through it. It awakens something wonderful and awful inside him. He devours it. Forgets everything. When he finally looks up, juice dripping from his chin, he sees his granddaughter, perched on a log, knees drawn up to her chin in utter fascination. 'That. Was. So disgusting.'

'Were you just watching me this whole time?'

'Bit hard not to.'

'I'm sorry. But I'm glad you didn't have any.'

'Clearly.' She leaps down and returns to her drawing, her masterplan. 'I probably would have had some, you know.'

'I'm glad you didn't. Your mother would have killed me.'

'She wouldn't have needed to find out.' He hears the threat but is too full to care. 'Now, may I see what you've been drawing?'

'I'm not quite finished.'

'Is any artist ever?'

'Yes. Me. I finish things.'

She moves back and forth across the site, making great arcs and violent dissections, bifurcating elaborately both nearby and far from the centre, where the fire, tended to every so often by her grandfather, pops and crackles. She goes about her business and he pretends to go about his, until she finally approaches him. She takes him by the hand and drags him through the dark up to the top of the small dune system, eroded beyond recovery, which overlooks their camp. From a vantage of just a few metres, the picture takes on a new life, lines forming into great cosmological meanings. Our solar system, there in the sand and soil.

The fire is the sun. The many small circles she swirled, the planets. The great ellipses she lassoed around the fire, their orbits. Between the orbits of what he thinks must be Mars and Jupiter, a frenzied ring of blemishes makes a great asteroid belt. And there, third rock from the fire, ludicrously expanded to allow for great detail, is our Earth. It moves him. He manages eventually to ask her if this is something she learned in the collective; she explains that she learns nothing at that school.

She then leads him back down, dragging him across the hazy band of stars into this quadrant of our galaxy so he can see it anew, up close. He takes in the oversized Earth, its continents and oceans all squished and rendered artfully in two dimensions. He does not bother to ask what is on the other side. A dozen or so dots mark cities. Berlin. New Amsterdam. Buenos Aires. Miami Pontoon. London. Toronto. Beijing. The rest he's not so sure of.

'I love it! What does it all mean?'

'Well, nothing really.'

'That's not true.' He shakes his head in wonder. 'Why these dots? These cities?'

'They are the places I'm going to go.'

He moves over to her, wraps his arms around her while he still can. The touch ties him to a memory of when she was only very little, shortly after their coming together. It's faint but true. Of her drawing something similar—stars and suns—in yellow and blue crayon on genuine paper sourced from a tree. She always giggled when he rolled out those old sheets for her to draw on. *Feels funny*, she would say, scratching her tiny fingernails along it.

He turns to her now, anxious. 'Why do you want to go out into the world?'

'Because I'm going to help it,' she says, fierce and certain in a way he could never know.

They ride in beneath the dying sky, tumbling down great breakers, working their oars as Evie taught them. Aloy glances back at her mother, guiding them through the narrow channels between the reefs, and knows.

She looks ahead. A dot in the distance, seated on the gumrest, slotted into the Earth. Grandfather.

As they glide in, sending a large wake rippling out over the shoal, she waves to him, holding up her catch for him to see. He beams, proud.

That night, circling the fire, huddling close as their kind have done since the beginning of time, they enjoy what they can. Together.

As always, the old man finds ways to walk back through time and stoke regret, prodding how it could have turned out otherwise; that there might still be some place, somewhere, that still has a chance.

But for Aloy this is just beginning.

Acknowledgements

I received support for *Children of Tomorrow* in so many special ways. I'm honoured to have been highly commended in the Victorian Premier's Literary Awards 2021 and to have received a Copyright Agency Cultural Fund to prepare an expanded version of the manuscript for Upswell Publishing. I would like to thank the eyes and ears along the way: James Bradley, Paul Dalgarno, Joey Eschrich, Jane Rawson, Alice Robinson, Kim Stanley Robinson, Veronica Sullivan, all of whom were generous enough to read or give advice. To the inimitable Terri-ann White at Upswell, it's hard to convey my delight in working and publishing with you. I could not be more thankful for the tireless work you and my editor, Julian Welch, put into this book. The existence of this book owes much to my agent Martin Shaw, who saw something worthwhile in *Children of Tomorrow*. Thank you for championing my work to the end and dragging it over the line.

Children of Tomorrow was born of my doctoral research in climate change communication. So it is appropriate to wind the clock back and thank those at both the University of Melbourne and Monash University who played a part in my path: Ali Alizadeh, Jarrod Hayes, Grace Moore, Philip Morrissey, Simone Murray, and, in particular, Chris Worth, for his exceedingly generous feedback over the years. To my friends and colleagues in the School of Media, Film and Journalism—Emily van der Nagel and Anastasia Kanjere—and the Monash Climate Change Communication Research Hub—James Goldie, Steph Hall, Remy Shergill, Tahnee Burgess, Ella Healy, John Cook, and Lucy Richardson—you guys are the best. To David Holmes, my associate supervisor and Director of the MCCCRH,

I owe a huge amount. Alongside David, I would like to thank the rest of my wonderful supervisory team, Kate Rigby, who was a guiding light from the very beginning, and Melinda Harvey, whose tireless work towards the end was especially appreciated.

Big cheers to my oldest mates, all of whom make the world a better place: Daniel Griffin, Elliot Yeatman, Louise Smith, Maleela Jullyan, and Nick Scott. More recent, but no less special people include Caz Platt, Cassia Menkhorst, Callum Mayling, Jon Ricketson and Paul Guardiani. To my doctoral buddies at Monash, thanks for the banter, in particular: Bec Bryson, Calvin Fung, Chloe Keel, Claire Moran, Brittany Ralph, Meg Randolph, Dave Reynolds, Nicki Ruslim, Shih Joo Tan, and Andrew Zammit. I need to single out two very special amigos—Ben Lyall and Pat Marple. Whatever luck brought us desk-to-desk at the start of our PhDs I am forever thankful for. You two are special in ways I cannot describe, so I won't even try.

Family ties this novel together. And so, Mum, Dad, thank you. I can't imagine how to repay you for the support you've given me. To my brothers, Dave and Rob, thank you for everything. We've been at various distances from one another over the years, but you've always felt close. To my sister-in-law Clare McCutcheon and my nephew Riley Milner, you are and always will be exceptionally dear to me. And to my English sister-in-law Beth Hallett-Milner, thanks for all the love and generosity you and Rob give, whether near or far away. To my brother-in-law Mitch and mother-in-law Catherine, aka 'Mimi', thanks for all the wonderful support—and a quiet space to write on occasions. Thanks to all my Sydney family, especially, Auntie Merry, Auntie Bev, Patrick Batchelor, Shannan Dodson, Charles Firth, Amanda Tattersall and Verity Firth. To my incredible family back in the UK, I'd like to thank you all. You're the best: Uncle Richard and Auntie Ann, Uncle Phil, Ciarán Milner and Ellie Isaacs, Liam Milner and Anna Buckler.

And Auntie Joyce (1953-2011), thank you for everything you gave me—I think you might have liked this one.

Finally, my little growing family. This has all been for you. Jess, the love we have makes every day on this warming world precious still. Thanks for putting up with me. It's over now, so on to the next adventure and forever. To Norah and Hadley, my children of tomorrow, there is no feeling so sacred as that which I feel for you. It's an endless love in a finite world; may it be an infinite resource for you.

J.R. BURGMANN is an emerging writer and critic. He is a graduate of the University of Melbourne and received his PhD in Literary and Cultural Studies from Monash University, where he is based at the Monash Climate Change Communication Research Hub. This debut novel was highly commended in the Victorian Premier's Literary Awards 2021 in the category of unpublished manuscripts. In 2022 he was awarded a Wheeler Centre Hot Desk Fellowship.